D0498173

How I Became
a Holy Mother

# How I Became
# a Holy Mother

## AND OTHER STORIES

Ruth Prawer Jhabvala

JOHN MURRAY

Acknowledgments are due to *The New Yorker*, *Cosmopolitan*, *The Cornhill Magazine* and *Encounter* in which these stories first appeared.

Photoset, printed and bound in Great Britain by REDWOOD BURN LIMITED Trowbridge & Esher

0 7195 3309 0

# CONTENTS

# HOW I BECAME A HOLY MOTHER

On my 23rd birthday when I was fed up with London and all the rest of it—boy friends, marriages (two), jobs (modelling), best friends that are suddenly your best enemies—I had this letter from my girl friend Sophie who was finding peace in an ashram in South India:

". . . oh Katie you wouldn't know me I'm such a changed person. I get up at 5—*a.m.*!!! I am an absolute vegetarian let alone no meat no eggs either and am making fabulous progress with my meditation. I have a special mantra of my own that Swamiji gave me at a special ceremony and I say it over and over in my mind. The sky here is blue all day long and I sit by the sea and watch the waves and have good thoughts . . ."

But by the time I got there Sophie had left—under a cloud, it seemed, though when I asked what she had done, they wouldn't tell me but only pursed their lips and looked sorrowful. I didn't stay long in that place. I didn't like the bitchy atmosphere, and that Swamiji was a big fraud, anyone could see that. I couldn't understand how a girl as sharp as Sophie had ever let herself be fooled by such a type. But I suppose if you want to be fooled you are. I found that out in some of the other ashrams I went to. There were some quite intelligent people in all of them but the way they just shut their eyes to certain things, it was incredible. It is not my rôle in life to criticise others so I kept quiet and went on to the

1

next place. I went to quite a few of them. These ashrams are a cheap way to live in India and there is always company and it isn't bad for a few days provided you don't get involved in their power politics. I was amazed to come across quite a few people I had known over the years and would never have expected to meet here. It is a shock when you see someone you had last met on the beach at St. Tropez now all dressed up in a saffron robe and meditating in some very dusty ashram in Madhya Pradesh. But really I could see their point because they were all as tired as I was of everything we had been doing and this certainly was different.

I enjoyed myself going from one ashram to the other and travelling all over India. Trains and buses are very crowded—I went third class, I had to be careful with my savings—but Indians can tell when you want to be left alone. They are very sensitive that way. I looked out of the window and thought my thoughts. After a time I became quite calm and rested. I hadn't brought too much stuff with me, but bit by bit I discarded most of that too till I had only a few things left that I could easily carry myself. I didn't even mind when my watch was pinched off me one night in a railway restroom (so-called). I felt myself to be a changed person. Once, at the beginning of my travels, there was a man sitting next to me on a bus who said he was an astrologer. He was a very sensitive and philosophical person—and I must say I was impressed by how many such one meets in India, quite ordinary people travelling third class. After we had been talking for a time and he had told me the future of India for the next 40 years, suddenly out of the blue he said to me "Madam, you have a very sad soul." It was true. I thought about it for days afterwards and cried a bit to myself. I did feel sad inside myself and heavy like with a stone. But as time went on and I

2

kept going round India—the sky always blue like Sophie had said, and lots of rivers and fields as well as desert—just quietly travelling and looking, I stopped feeling like that. Now I was as a matter of fact quite light inside as if that stone had gone.

Then I stopped travelling and stayed in this one place instead. I liked it better than any of the other ashrams for several reasons. One of them was that the scenery was very picturesque. This cannot be said of all ashrams as many of them seem to be in sort of dust bowls, or in the dirtier parts of very dirty holy cities or even cities that aren't holy at all but just dirty. But this ashram was built on the slope of a mountain, and behind it there were all the other mountains stretching right up to the snow-capped peaks of the Himalayas; and on the other side it ran down to the river which I will not say can have been very clean (with all those pilgrims dipping in it) but certainly looked clean from up above and not only clean but as clear and green as the sky was clear and blue. Also along the bank of the river there were many little pink temples with pink cones and they certainly made a pretty scene. Inside the ashram also the atmosphere was good which again cannot be said of all of them, far from it. But the reason the atmosphere was good here was because of the head of this ashram who was called Master. They are always called something like that—if not Swamiji then Maharaj-ji or Babaji or Maharishiji or Guruji; but this one was just called plain Master, in English.

He was full of pep and go. Early in the morning he would say "Well what shall we do today!" and then plan some treat like all of us going for a swim in the river with a picnic lunch to follow. He didn't want anyone to have a dull moment or to fall into a depression which I suppose many there were apt to

3

do, left to their own devices. In some ways he reminded me of those big business types that sometimes (in other days!) took me out to dinner. They too had that kind of superhuman energy and seemed to be stronger than other people. I forgot to say that Master was a big burly man, and as he didn't wear all that many clothes—usually only a loincloth—you could see just how big and burly he was. His head was large too and it was completely shaven so that it looked even larger. He wasn't ugly, not at all. Or perhaps if he was one forgot about it very soon because of all that dynamism.

As I said, the ashram was built on the slope of a mountain. I don't think it was planned at all but had just grown: there was one little room next to the other and the Meditation Hall and the dining hall and Master's quarters—whatever was needed was added and it all ran higgledy-piggledy down the mountain. I had one of the little rooms to myself and made myself very snug in there. The only furniture provided by the ashram was one string bed, but I bought a handloom rug from the Lepers Rehabilitation Centre and I also put up some pictures, like a Tibetan Mandala which was very colourful. Everyone liked my room and wanted to come and spend time there, but I was a bit cagey about that as I needed my privacy. I always had lots to do, like writing letters or washing my hair and I was also learning to play the flute. So I was quite happy and independent and didn't really need company though there was plenty of it, if and when needed.

There were Master's Indian disciples who were all learning to be swamis. They wanted to renounce the world and had shaved their heads and wore an orange sort of toga thing. When they were ready, Master was going to make them into full swamis. Most of these junior swamis were very young—

4

just boys, some of them—but even those that weren't all that young were certainly so at heart. Sometimes they reminded me of a lot of school kids, they were so full of tricks and fun. But I think basically they were very serious—they couldn't not be, considering how they were renouncing and were supposed to be studying all sorts of very difficult things. The one I liked the best was called Vishwa. I liked him not only because he was the best looking, which he undoubtedly was, but I felt he had a lot going for him. Others said so too—in fact, they all said that Vishwa was the most advanced and was next in line for full initiation. I always let him come and talk to me in my room whenever he wanted to, and we had some interesting conversations.

Then there were Master's foreign disciples. They weren't so different from the other Europeans and Americans I had met in other ashrams except that the atmosphere here was so much better and that made them better too. They didn't have to fight with each other over Master's favours—I'm afraid that was very much the scene in some of the other ashrams which were like harems, the way they were all vying for the favour of their guru. But Master never encouraged that sort of relationship, and although of course many of them did have very strong attachments to him, he managed to keep them all healthy. And that's really saying something because, like in all the other ashrams, many of them were not healthy people; through no fault of their own quite often, they had just had a bad time and were trying to get over it.

Once Master said to me "What about you, Katie?" This was when I was alone with him in his room. He had called me in for some dictation—we were all given little jobs to do for him from time to time, to keep us busy and happy I suppose. Just let me say a few words about his room and get it over

5

with. It was *awful*. It had linoleum on the floor of the nastiest pattern, and green strip lighting, and the walls were painted green too and had been decorated with calendars and pictures of what were supposed to be gods and saints but might as well have been Bombay film stars, they were so fat and gaudy. Master and all the junior swamis were terribly proud of this room. Whenever he acquired anything new—like some plastic flowers in a hideous vase—he would call everyone to admire and was so pleased and complacent that really it was not possible to say anything except "Yes very nice."

When he said "What about you, Katie?" I knew at once what he meant. That was another thing about him—he would suddenly come out with something as if there had already been a long talk between you on this subject. So when he asked me that, it was like the end of a conversation, and all I had to do was think for a moment and then I said "I'm okay." Because that was what he had asked: was I okay? Did I want anything, any help or anything? And I didn't. I really was okay now. I hadn't always been but I got so travelling around on my own and then being in this nice place here with him.

This was before the Countess came. Once she was there, everything was rather different. For weeks before her arrival people started talking about her: she was an important figure there, and no wonder since she was very rich and did a lot for the ashram and for Master when he went abroad on his lecture tours. I wondered what she was like. When I asked Vishwa about her, he said "She is a great spiritual lady."

We were both sitting outside my room. There was a little open space round which several other rooms were grouped. One of these—the biggest, at the corner—was being got ready for the Countess. It was the one that was always kept for her. People were vigorously sweeping in there and scrubbing the floor with soap and water.

"She is rich and from very aristocratic family," Vishwa said, "but when she met Master she was ready to give up everything." He pointed to the room which was being scrubbed: "This is where she stays. And see—not even a bed—she sleeps on the floor like a holy person. Oh Katie, when someone like me gives up the world, what is there? It is not such a great thing. But when *she* does it—" His face glowed. He had very bright eyes and a lovely complexion. He always looked very pure, owing no doubt to the very pure life he led.

Of course I got more and more curious about her, but when she came I was disappointed. I had expected her to be very special, but the only special thing about her was that I should meet her *here*. Otherwise she was a type I had often come across at posh parties and in the salons where I used to model. And the way she walked towards me and said "Welcome!"—she might as well have been walking across a carpet in a salon. She had a full-blown, middleaged figure (she must have been in her fifties) but very thin legs on which she took long strides with her toes turned out. She gave me a deep searching look—and that too I was used to from someone like her because very worldly people always do that: to find out who you are and how usable. But in her case now I suppose it was to search down into my soul and see what that was like.

I don't know what her conclusion was, but I must have passed because she was always kind to me and even asked for my company quite often. Perhaps this was partly because we lived across from each other and she suffered from insomnia

7

and needed someone to talk to at night. I'm a sound sleeper myself and wasn't always very keen when she came to wake me. But she would nag me till I got up. "Come on, Katie, be a sport," she would say. She used many English expressions like that: she spoke English very fluently though with a funny accent. I heard her speak to the French and Italian and German people in the ashram very fluently in their languages too. I don't know what nationality she herself was—a sort of mixture I think—but of course people like her have been everywhere, not to mention their assorted governesses when young.

She always made me come into her room. She said mine was too *luxurious*, she didn't feel right in it as she had given up all that. Hers certainly wasn't luxurious. Like Vishwa had said, there wasn't a stick of furniture in it and she slept on the floor on a mat. As the electricity supply in the ashram was very fitful, we usually sat by candlelight. It was queer sitting like that with her on the floor with a stub of candle between us. I didn't have to do much talking as she did it all. She used her arms a lot, in sweeping gestures, and I can still see them weaving around there by candlelight as if she was doing a dance with them; and her eyes which were big and baby-blue were stretched wide open in wonder at everything she was telling me. Her life was like a fairy tale, she said. She gave me all the details though I can't recall them as I kept dropping off to sleep (naturally at two in the morning). From time to time she'd stop and say sharply "Are you asleep, Katie," and then she would poke me till I said no I wasn't. She told me how she first met Master at a lecture he had come to give in Paris. At the end of the lecture she went up to him—she said she had to elbow her way through a crowd of women all try-ing to get near him—and simply bowed down at his feet. No

8

words spoken. There had been no need. It had been predestined.

She was also very fond of Vishwa. It seemed all three of them—i.e. her, Master, and Vishwa—had been closely related to each other in several previous incarnations. I think they had been either her sons or her husbands or fathers, I can't remember which exactly but it was very close so it was no wonder she felt about them the way she did. She had big plans for Vishwa. He was to go abroad and be a spiritual leader. She and Master often talked about it, and it was fascinating listening to them, but there was one thing I couldn't understand and that was why did it have to be Vishwa and not Master who was to be a spiritual leader in the West? I'd have thought Master himself had terrific qualifications for it.

Once I asked them. We were sitting in Master's room and the two of them were talking about Vishwa's future. When I asked "What about Master?" she gave a dramatic laugh and pointed at him like she was accusing him: "Ask him! Why don't you ask him!"

He gave a guilty smile and shifted around a bit on his throne. I say throne—it really was that: he received everyone in this room so a sort of dais had been fixed up at one end and a deer-skin spread on it for him to sit on; loving disciples had painted an arched back to the dais and decorated it with stars and symbols stuck on in silver paper (hideous!).

When she saw him smile like that, she really got exasperated. "If you knew, Katie," she said, "how I have argued with him, how I have fought, how I have begged and pleaded on my *knees*. But he is as stubborn as—as—"

"A mule," he kindly helped her out.

"Forgive me," she said (because you can't call your guru

9

names, that just isn't done!); though next moment she had worked herself up again: "Do you know," she asked me, "how many people were waiting for him at the airport last time he went to New York? Do you know how many came to his lectures? That they had to be turned away from the *door* till we took a bigger hall! And not to speak of those who came to enrol for the special 3-week Meditation-via-Contemplation course."

"She is right," he said. "They are very kind to me."

"Kind! They want him—need him—are crazy with love and devotion—"

"It's all true," he said. "But the trouble is, you see, I'm a very, very lazy person." And as he said this, he gave a big yawn and stretched himself to prove how lazy he was: but he didn't look it—on the contrary, when he stretched like that, pushing out his big chest, he looked like he was humming with energy.

That evening he asked me to go for a stroll with him. We walked by the river which was very busy with people dipping in it for religious reasons. The temples were also busy—whenever we passed one, they seemed to be bursting in there with hymns, and cymbals, and little bells.

Master said: "It is true that everyone is very kind to me in the West. Oh they make a big fuss when I come. They have even made a song for me—it goes—wait, let me see—"

He stopped still and several people took the opportunity to come up to ask for his blessing. There were many other holy men walking about but somehow Master stood out. Some of the holy men also came up to be blessed by him.

"Yes it goes: '*He's here! Our Master ji is here Jai jai Master! Jai jai He!*' They stand waiting for me at the airport, and when I come out of the customs they burst into song. They

10

carry big banners and also have drums and flutes. What a noise they make! Some of them begin to dance there and then on the spot, they are so happy. And everyone stares and looks at me, all the respectable people at the airport, and they wonder 'Now who is this ruffian?' "

He had to stop again because a shopkeeper came running out of his stall to crouch at Master's feet. He was the grocer—everyone knew he used false weights—as well as the local moneylender and the biggest rogue in town, but when Master blessed him I could see tears come in his eyes, he felt so good.

"A car has been bought for my use," Master said when we walked on again. "Also a lease has been taken on a beautiful residence in New Hampshire. Now they wish to buy an aeroplane to enable me to fly from coast to coast." He sighed. "She is right to be angry with me. But what am I to do? I stand in the middle of Times Square or Piccadilly, London, and I look up and there are all the beautiful beautiful buildings stretching so high up into heaven: yes I look at them but it is not them I see at all, Katie! Not them at all!"

He looked up and I with him, and I understood that what he saw in Times Square and Piccadilly was what we saw now—all those mountains growing higher and higher above the river, and some of them so high that you couldn't make out whether it was them, with snow on top or the sky with clouds in it.

Before the Countess' arrival, everything had been very easy-going. We usually did our meditation, but if we happened to miss out, it never mattered too much. Also there was a lot of sitting around gossiping or trips to the bazaar for cats. But the Countess put us on a stricter régime. Now we all had

11

a time-table to follow, and there were gongs and bells going off all day to remind us. This started at 5 a.m. when it was meditation time, followed by purificatory bathing time, and study time, and discussion time, and hymn time, and so on till lights-out time. Throughout the day disciples could be seen making their way up or down the mountain-side as they passed from one group activity to the other. If there was any delay in the schedule, the Countess got impatient and clapped her hands and chivied people along. The way she herself clambered up and down the mountain was just simply amazing for someone her age. Sometimes she went right to the top of the ashram where there was a pink plaster pillar inscribed with Golden Rules for Golden Living (a sort of Indian Ten Commandments): from here she could look all round, survey her domain as it were. When she wanted to summon everyone, she climbed up there with a pair of cymbals and how she beat them together! Boom! Bang! She must have had military blood in her veins, probably German.

She had drawn up a very strict time-table for Vishwa to cover every aspect of his education. He had to learn all sorts of things; not only English and a bit of French and German, but also how to use a knife and fork and even how to address people by their proper titles in case ambassadors and big church people and such were drawn into the movement as was fully expected. Because I'd been a model, I was put in charge of his deportment. I was supposed to teach him how to walk and sit nicely. He had to come to my room for lessons in the afternoons, and it was quite fun though I really didn't know what to teach him. As far as I was concerned, he was more graceful than anyone I'd ever seen. I loved the way he sat on the floor with his legs tucked under him; he could sit like that without moving for hours and hours. Or he might lie full length on the floor with his head supported on one hand and his ascetic's robe falling in folds round him so that he looked like a piece of sculpture you might see in a museum. I forgot to say that the Countess had decided he wasn't to shave his hair any more like the other junior swamis but was to grow it and have long curls. It wasn't long yet but it was certainly curly and framed his face very prettily.

After the first few days we gave up having lessons and just talked and spent our time together. He sat on the rug and I on the bed. He told me the story of his life and I told him mine. But his was much better than mine. His father had been the station master at some very small junction, and the family lived in a little railway house near enough the tracks to run and put the signals up or down as required. Vishwa had plenty of brothers and sisters to play with, and friends at the little school he went to at the other end of town; but quite often he felt like not being with anyone. He would set off to school with his copies and pencils like everyone else, but half way he would change his mind and take another turning that led out of town into some open fields. Here he would lie down under a tree and look at patches of sky through the leaves of the tree, and the leaves moving ever so gently if there was a breeze or some birds shook their wings in there. He would stay all day and in the evening go home and not tell anyone. His mother was a religious person who regularly visited the temple and sometimes he went with her but he never felt anything special. Then Master came to town and gave a lecture in a tent that was put up for him on the Parade Ground. Vishwa went with his mother to hear him, again not expecting anything special, but the moment he saw Master something very peculiar happened: he couldn't quite describe it, but he said it was like when there is a wedding on

13

a dark night and the fireworks start and there are those that shoot up into the sky and then burst into a huge white fountain of light scattering sparks all over so that you are blinded and dazzled with it. It was like that, Vishwa said. Then he just went away with Master. His family were sad at first to lose him, but they were proud too like all families are when one of them renounces the world to become a holy man.

Those were good afternoons we had, and we usually took the precaution of locking the door so no one could interrupt us. If we heard the Countess coming—one good thing about her, you could always *hear* her a mile off, she never moved an inch without shouting instructions to someone—the moment we heard her we'd jump up and unlock the door and fling it wide open: so when she looked in, she could see us having our lesson—Vishwa walking up and down with a book on his head, or sitting like on a dais to give a lecture and me showing him what to do with his hands.

When I told him the story of *my* life, we both cried. Especially when I told him about my first marriage when I was only 16 and Danny just 20. He was a bass player in a group and he was really good and would have got somewhere if he hadn't freaked out. It was terrible seeing him do that, and the way he treated me after those first six months we had together which were out of this world. I never had anything like that with anyone ever again, though I got involved with many people afterwards. Everything just got worse and worse till I reached an all-time low with my second marriage which was to a company director (so-called, though don't ask me what sort of company) and a very smooth operator indeed besides being a sadist. Vishwa couldn't stand it when I came to that part of my story. He begged me not to go on, he put his hands over his ears. We weren't in my room that time

14

but on top of the ashram by the Pillar of the Golden Rules. The view from here was fantastic, and it was so high up that you felt you might as well be in heaven, especially at this hour of the evening when the sky was turning all sorts of colours though mostly gold from the sun setting in it. Everything I was telling Vishwa seemed very far away. I can't say it was as if it had never happened, but it seemed like it had happened in someone else's life. There were tears on Vishwa's lashes, and I couldn't help myself, I had to kiss them away. After which we kissed properly. His mouth was as soft as a flower and his breath as sweet; of course he had never tasted meat nor eaten anything except the purest food such as a lamb might eat.

The door of my room was not the only one that was locked during those hot afternoons. Quite a few of the foreign disciples locked theirs for purposes I never cared to enquire into. At first I used to pretend to myself they were sleeping, and afterwards I didn't care what they were doing. I mean, even if they weren't sleeping, I felt there was something just as good and innocent about what they actually *were* doing. And after a while—when we had told each other the story of our respective lives and had run out of conversation—Vishwa and I began to do it too. This was about the time when preparations were going on for his final Renunciation and Initiation ceremony. It's considered the most important day in the life of a junior swami, when he ceases to be junior and becomes a senior or proper swami. It's a very solemn ceremony. A funeral pyre is lit and his junior robe and his caste thread are burned on it. All this is symbolic—it means he's dead to the world but resurrected to the spiritual life. In Vishwa's case, his resurrection was a bit different from the usual. He wasn't fitted out in the standard senior swami

15

outfit—which is a piece of orange cloth and a begging bowl—but instead the Countess dressed him up in the clothes he was to wear in the West. She had herself designed a white silk robe for him, together with accessories like beads, sandals, the deer skin he was to sit on, and an embroidered shawl.

Getting all this ready meant many trips to the bazaar, and often she made Vishwa and me go with her. She swept through the bazaar the same way she did through the ashram, and the shopkeepers leaned eagerly out of their stalls to offer their salaams which she returned or not as they happened to be standing in her books. She was pretty strict with all of them—but most of all with the tailor whose job it was to stitch Vishwa's new silk robes. We spent hours in his little shop while Vishwa had to stand there and be fitted. The tailor crouched at his feet, stitching and restitching the hem to the Countess' instructions. She and I would stand back and look at Vishwa with our heads to one side while the tailor waited anxiously for her verdict. Ten to one she would say "No! Again!"

But once she said not to the tailor but to me "Vishwa stands very well now. He has a good pose."

"Not bad," I said, continuing to look critically at Vishwa and in such a way that he had a job not to laugh.

What she said next however killed all desire for laughter: "I think we could end the deportment lessons now," and then she shouted at the tailor: "What is this! What are you doing! What sort of monkey-work do you call that!"

I managed to persuade her that I hadn't finished with Vishwa yet and there were still a few tricks of the trade I had to teach him. But I knew it was a short reprieve and that soon our lessons would have to end. Also plans were now afoot for

16

Vishwa's departure. He was to go with the Countess when she returned to Europe in a few weeks time; and she was already very busy corresponding with her contacts in various places, and all sorts of lectures and meetings were being arranged. But that wasn't the only thing worrying me: what was even worse was the change I felt taking place in Vishwa himself, especially after his Renunciation and Initiation ceremony. I think he was getting quite impressed with himself. The Countess made a point of treating him as if he were a guru already, and she bowed to him the same way she did to Master. And of course whatever she did everyone else followed suit, specially the foreign disciples. I might just say that they're always keen on things like that—I mean, bowing down and touching feet—I don't know what kick they get out of it but they do, the Countess along with the rest. Most of them do it very clumsily—not like Indians who are *born* to it—so sometimes you feel like laughing when you look at them. But they're always very solemn about it and afterwards, when they stumble up again, there's a sort of holy glow on their faces. Vishwa looked down at them with a benign expression and he also got into the habit of blessing them the way Master did.

Now I stayed alone in the afternoons, feeling very miserable, specially when I thought of what was going on in some of the other rooms and how happy people were in there. After a few days of this I couldn't stand being on my own and started wandering around looking for company. But the only person up and doing at that time of day was the Countess who I didn't particularly want to be with. So I went and sat in Master's room where the door was always open in case any of us needed him any time. Like everybody else, he was often

17

asleep that time of afternoon but it didn't matter. Just being in his presence was good. I sat on one of the green plastic benches that were ranged round his room and looked at him sleeping which he did sitting upright on his throne. Quite suddenly he would open his eyes and look straight at me and say "Ah Katie" as if he'd known all along that I was sitting there.

One day there was an awful commotion outside. Master woke up as the Countess came in with two foreign disciples, a boy and a girl, who stood hanging their heads while she told us what she had caught them doing. They were two very young disciples; I think the boy didn't even have to shave yet. One couldn't imagine them doing anything really evil, and Master didn't seem to think so. He just told them to go away and have their afternoon rest. But because the Countess was very upset he tried to comfort her which he did by telling about his early life in the world when he was a married man. It had been an arranged marriage of course, and his wife had been very young, just out of school. Being married for them had been like a game, specially the cooking and housekeeping part which she had enjoyed very much. Every Sunday she had dressed up in a spangled sari and high-heeled shoes and he had escorted her on the bus to the cinema where they stood in a queue for the one-rupee seats. He had loved her more than he had ever loved anyone or anything in all his life and had not thought it possible to love so much. But it only lasted two years at the end of which time she died of a miscarriage. He left his home then and wandered about for many years, doing all sorts of different jobs. He worked as a motor mechanic, and a salesman for medical supplies, and had even been in films for a while on the distribution side. But not finding rest anywhere, he finally decided to give up

18

the world. He explained to us that it had been the only logical thing to do. Having learned during his two years of marriage how happy it was possible for a human being to be, he was never again satisfied to settle for anything less; but also seeing how it couldn't last on a worldly plane, he had decided to look for it elsewhere and help other people to do so with him.

I liked what he said, but I don't think the Countess took much of it in. She was more in her own thoughts. She was silent and gloomy which was *very* unusual for her. When she woke me that night for her midnight confessions, she seemed quite a different person: and now she didn't talk about her fairy tale life or her wonderful plans for the future but on the contrary about all the terrible things she had suffered in the past. She went right back to the time she was in her teens and had eloped with and married an old man, a friend of her father's, and from there on it was all just one long terrible story of bad marriages and unhappy love affairs and other sufferings that I wished I didn't have to listen to. But I couldn't leave her in the state she was in. She was crying and sobbing and lying face down on the ground. It was eerie in that bare cell of hers with the one piece of candle flickering in the wind which was very strong, and the rain beating down like fists on the tin roof.

The monsoon had started, and when you looked up now, there weren't any mountains left, only clouds hanging down very heavily; and when you looked down, the river was also heavy and full. Every day there were stories of pilgrims drowning in it, and one night it washed over one bank and swept away a little colony of huts that the lepers had built for themselves. Now they no longer sat sunning themselves on the bridge but were carted away to the infectious diseases hospital. The rains came gushing down the mountain right

19

into the ashram so that we were all wading ankle-deep in mud and water. Many rooms were flooded and their occupants had to move into other people's rooms resulting in personality clashes. Everyone bore grudges and took sides so that it became rather like the other ashrams I had visited and not liked.

The person who changed the most was the Countess. Although she was still dashing up and down the mountain, it was no longer to get the place in running order. Now she tucked up her skirts to wade from room to room to peer through chinks and see what people were up to. She didn't trust anyone but appointed herself as a one-man spying organisation. She even suspected Master and me! At least me—she asked me what I went to his room for in the afternoon and sniffed at my reply in a way I didn't care for. After that one awful outburst she had, she didn't call me at night any more but she was certainly after me during the day.

She guarded Vishwa like a dragon. She wouldn't even let me pass his room, and if she saw me going anywhere in that direction, she'd come running to tell me to take the other way round. I wasn't invited any more to accompany them to the bazaar but only she and Vishwa set off, with her holding a big black umbrella over them both. If they happened to pass me on the way, she would tilt the umbrella so he wouldn't be able to see me. Not that this was necessary as he never seemed to see me anyway. His eyes were always lowered and the expression on his face very serious. He had stopped joking around with the junior swamis, which I suppose was only fitting now he was a senior swami as well as about to become a spiritual leader. The Countess had fixed up a throne for him at the end of Master's room so he wouldn't have to sit on the floor and the benches along with

20

the rest of us. When we all got together in there, Master would be at one end on his throne and Vishwa at the other on his. At Master's end there was always lots going on—everyone laughing and Master making jokes and having his fun—but Vishwa just sat very straight in the lotus pose and never looked at anyone or spoke, and only when the Countess pushed people to go and touch his feet, he'd raise a hand to bless them.

With the rains came flies and mosquitoes, and people began to fall sick with all sorts of mysterious fevers. The Countess—who was terrified of germs and had had herself pumped full of every kind of injection before coming to India—was now in a great hurry to be off with Vishwa. But before they could leave, he too came down with one of those fevers. She took him at once into her own room and kept him isolated in there with everything shut tight. She wouldn't let any of us near him. But I peeped in through the chinks, not caring whether she saw me or not. I even pleaded with her to let me come in, and once she let me but only to look at him from the door while she stood guard by his pillow. His eyes were shut and he was breathing heavily and moaning in an awful way. The Countess said I could go now, but instead I rushed up to Vishwa's bed. She tried to get between us but I pushed her out of the way and got down by the bed and held him where he lay moaning with his eyes shut. The Countess shrieked and pulled at me to get me away. I was shrieking too. We must have sounded and looked like a couple of madwomen. Vishwa opened his eyes and when he saw me there and moreover found that he was in my arms, *he* began to shriek too, as if he was frightened of me and that perhaps I was the very person he was having those terrible fever dreams about that made him groan.

21

It may have been this accidental shock treatment but that night Vishwa's fever came down and he began to get better. Master announced that there was going to be a Yagna or prayer-meet to give thanks for Vishwa's recovery. It was to be a really big show. Hordes of helpers came up from the town, all eager to take part in this event so as to benefit from the spiritual virtue it was expected to generate. The Meditation Hall was repainted salmon pink and the huge holy *OM* sign at one end of it was lit up all round with coloured bulbs that flashed on and off. Everyone worked with a will, and apparently good was already beginning to be generated because the rains stopped, the mud lanes in the ashram dried up, and the river flowed back into its banks. The disciples stopped quarrelling which may have been partly due to the fact that everyone could move back into their own rooms.

The Countess and Vishwa kept going down into the town to finish off with the tailors and embroiderers. They also went to the printer who was making large posters to be sent abroad to advertise Vishwa's arrival. The Countess often asked me to go with them: she was really a good-natured person and did not want me to feel left out. Especially now that she was sure there wasn't a dangerous situation working up between me and Vishwa. There she was right. I wasn't in the least interested in him and felt that the less I saw of him the better. I couldn't forget the way he had shrieked that night in the Countess' room as if I was something impure and dreadful. But on the contrary to me it seemed that it had been *he* who was impure and dreadful with his fever dreams. I didn't even like to think what went on in them.

The Great Yagna began and it really was great. The Meditation Hall was packed and was terribly hot not only with all the people there but also because of the sacrificial

22

flames that sizzled as more and more clarified butter was poured on them amid incantations. Everyone was smiling and singing and sweating. Master was terrific—he was right by the fire stark naked except for the tiniest bit of loincloth. His chest glistened with oil and seemed to reflect the flames leaping about. Sometimes he jumped up on his throne and waved his arms to make everyone join in louder; and when they did, he got so happy he did a little jig standing up there. Vishwa was on the other side of the Hall also on a throne. He was half reclining in his spotless white robe; he did not seem to feel the heat at all but lay there as if made out of cool marble. He reminded me of the god Shiva resting on top of his snowy mountain. The Countess sat near him, and I saw how she tried to talk to him once or twice but he took no notice of her. After a while she got up and went out which was not surprising for it really was not her scene, all that noise and singing and the neon lights and decorations.

It went on all night. No one seemed to get tired—they just got more and more worked up and the singing got louder and the fire hotter. Other people too began to do little jigs like Master's. I left the Hall and walked around by myself. It was a fantastic night, the sky sprinkled all over with stars and a moon like a melon. When I passed the Countess' door, she called me in. She was lying on her mat on the floor and said she had a migraine. No wonder, with all that noise. I liked it myself but I knew that, though she was very much attracted to Eastern religions, her taste in music was more for the Western classical type (she loved string quartets and had had a long *affaire* with a cellist). She confessed to me that she was very anxious to leave now and get Vishwa started on his career. I think she would have liked to confess more things, but I had to get on. I made my way uphill past all the

23

different buildings till I had reached the top of the ashram and the Pillar of the Golden Rules. Here I stood and looked down.

I saw the doors of the Meditation Hall open and Master and Vishwa come out. They were lit up by the lights from the Hall. Master was big and black and naked except for his triangle of orange cloth, and Vishwa was shining in white. I saw Master raise his arm and point it up, up to the top of the ashram. The two of them reminded me of a painting I've seen of I think it was an angel pointing out a path to a pilgrim. And like a pilgrim Vishwa began to climb up the path that Master had shown him. I stood by the Pillar of the Golden Rules and waited for him. When he got to me, we didn't have to speak one word. He was like a charged dynamo; I'd never known him like that. It was more like it might have been with Master instead of Vishwa. The drums and hymns down in the Meditation Hall also reached their crescendo just then. Of course Vishwa was too taken up with what he was doing to notice anything going on round him, so it was only me that saw the Countess come uphill. She was walking quite slowly and I suppose I could have warned Vishwa in time but it seemed a pity to interrupt him, so I just let her come on up and find us.

Master finally settled everything to everyone's satisfaction. He said Vishwa and I were to be a couple, and whereas Vishwa was to be the Guru, I was to embody the Mother principle (which is also very important). Once she caught on to the idea, the Countess rather liked it. She designed an outfit for me too—a sort of flowing white silk robe, really quite becoming. You might have seen posters of Vishwa and me together, both of us in these white robes, his hair black and

24

curly, mine blonde and straight. I suppose we do make a good couple—anyway, people seem to like us and to get something out of us. We do our best. It's not very hard; mostly we just have to sit there and radiate. The results are quite satisfactory—I mean the effect we seem to have on people who need it. The person who really has to work hard is the Countess because she has to look after all the business and organisational end. We have a strenuous tour programme. Sometimes it's like being on a one-night stand and doing your turn and then packing up in a hurry to get to the next one. Some of the places we stay in aren't too good—motels where you have to pay in advance in case you flit—and when she is very tired, the Countess wrings her hands and says "My God, what am I doing here?" It must be strange for her who's been used to all the grand hotels everywhere, but of course really she likes it. It's her life's fulfilment. But for Vishwa and me it's just a job we do, and all the time we want to be somewhere else and are thinking of that other place. I often remember what Master told me, what happened to him when he looked up in Times Square and Piccadilly, and it's beginning to happen to me too. I seem to *see* those mountains and the river and temples; and then I long to be there.

# IN THE MOUNTAINS

When one lives alone for most of the time and meets almost nobody, then care for one's outward appearance tends to drop away. That was what happened to Pritam. As the years went by and she continued living by herself, her appearance became rougher and shabbier, and though she was still in her thirties, she completely forgot to care for herself or think about herself as a physical person.

Her mother was just the opposite. She was plump and pampered, loved pastries and silk saris, and always smelled of lavender. Pritam smelled of—what was it? Her mother, enfolded in Pritam's embrace after a separation of many months, found herself sniffing in an attempt to identify the odour emanating from her. Perhaps it was from Pritam's clothes, which she probably did not change as frequently as was desirable. Tears came to the mother's eyes. They were partly for what her daughter had become and partly for the happiness of being with her again.

Pritam thumped her on the back. Her mother always cried at their meetings and at their partings. Pritam usually could not help being touched by these tears, even though she was aware of the mixed causes that evoked them. Now, to hide her own feelings, she became gruffer and more manly, and even gave the old lady a push toward a chair. "Go on, sit down," she said. "I suppose you are dying for your cup of tea." She had it all ready, and the mother took it gratefully, for she loved and needed tea, and the journey up from the

26

plains had greatly tired her.

But she could not drink with enjoyment. Pritam's tea was always too strong for her—a black country brew such as peasants drank, and the milk was also that of peasants, too newly rich and warm from the buffalo. And they were in this rough and barely furnished room in the rough stone house perched on the mountainside. And there was Pritam herself. The mother had to concentrate all her energies on struggling against more tears.

"I suppose you don't like the tea," Pritam said challengingly. She watched severely while the mother proved herself by drinking it up to the last drop, and Pritam refilled the cup. She asked, "How is everybody? Same as usual? Eating, making money?"

"No, no," said the mother, not so much denying the fact that this was what the family was doing as protesting against Pritam's saying so.

"Aren't they going up to Simla this year?"

"On Thursday," the mother said, and shifted uncomfortably.

"And stopping here?"

"Yes. For lunch."

The mother kept her eyes lowered. She said nothing more, though there was more to say. It would have to wait till a better hour. Let Pritam first get over the prospect of entertaining members of her family for a few hours on Thursday. It was nothing new or unexpected, for some of them stopped by every year on their way farther up the mountains. However much they may have desired to do so, they couldn't just drive past; it wouldn't be decent. But the prospect of meeting held no pleasure for anyone. Quite often there was a quarrel, and then Pritam cursed them as they drove away, and they sighed

27

at the necessity of keeping up family relationships, instead of having their lunch comfortably in the hotel a few miles farther on.

Pritam said, "I suppose you will be going with them," and went on at once, "Naturally, why should you stay? What is there for you here?"

"I want to stay."

"No, you love to be in Simla. It's so nice and jolly, and meeting everyone walking on the Mall, and tea in Davico's. Nothing like that here. You even hate my tea."

"I want to stay with you."

"But I don't want you!" Pritam was laughing, not angry. "You will be in my way, and then how will I carry on all my big love affairs?"

"What, what?"

Pritam clapped her hands in delight. "Oh no. I'm telling you nothing, because then you will want to stay and you will scare everyone away." She gave her mother a sly look and added, "You will scare poor Doctor Sahib away."

"Oh Doctor Sahib," said the old lady, relieved to find it had all been a joke. But she continued with disapproval, "Does he still come here?"

"Well, what do you think?" Pritam stopped laughing now and became offended. "If he doesn't come, then who will come? Except some goats and monkeys, perhaps. I know he is not good enough for you. You don't like him to come here. You would prefer me to know only goats and monkeys. And the family, of course."

"When did I say I don't like him?" the mother said.

"People don't have to say. And other people are quite capable of feeling without anyone saying. Here." Pritam snatched up her mother's cup and filled it, with rather a

28

vengeful air, for the third time.

Actually, it wasn't true that the mother disliked Doctor Sahib. He came to visit the next morning, and as soon as she saw him she had her usual sentiment about him—not dislike but disapproval. He certainly did not look like a person fit to be on terms of social intercourse with any member of her family. He was a tiny man, shabby and even dirty. He wore a kind of suit, but it was in a terrible condition and so were his shoes. One eye of his spectacles, for some reason, was blacked out with a piece of cardboard.

"Ah!" he exclaimed when he saw her. "Mother has come!" And he was so genuinely happy that her disapproval could not stand up to him—at least, not entirely.

"Mother brings us tidings and good cheer from the great world outside," Doctor Sahib went on. "What are we but two mountain hermits? Or I could even say two mountain bears."

He sat at a respectful distance away from the mother, who was ensconced in a basket chair. She had come to sit in the garden. There was a magnificent view from here of the plains below and the mountains above; however, she had not come out to enjoy the scenery but to get the benefit of the morning sun. Although it was the height of summer, she always felt freezing cold inside the house, which seemed like a stone tomb.

"Has Madam told you about our winter?" Doctor Sahib said. "Oh, what these two bears have gone through! Ask her."

"His roof fell in," Pritam said.

"One night I was sleeping in my bed. Suddenly—what shall I tell you—crash, bang! Boom and bang! To me it seemed that all the mountains were falling and, let alone the

29

mountains, heaven itself was coming down into my poor house. I said, 'Doctor Sahib, your hour has come.'"

"I told him, I told him all summer, 'The first snowfall and your roof will fall in.' And when it happened all he could do was stand there and wring his hands. What an idiot!"

"If it hadn't been for Madam, God knows what would have become of me. But she took me in and all winter she allowed me to have my corner by her own fireside."

The mother looked at them with startled eyes.

"Oh yes, all winter," Pritam said, mocking her. "And all alone, just the two of us. Why did you have to tell her?" she reproached Doctor Sahib. "Now she is shocked. Just look at her face. She is thinking we are two guilty lovers."

The mother flushed, and so did Doctor Sahib. An expression of bashfulness came into his face, mixed with regret, with melancholy. He was silent for some time, his head lowered. Then he said to the mother, "Look, can you see it?" He pointed at his house, which nestled farther down the mountainside, some way below Pritam's. It was a tiny house, not much more than a hut. "All hale and hearty again. Madam had the roof fixed, and now I am snug and safe once more in my own little kingdom."

Pritam said, "One day the whole place is going to come down, not just the roof, and then what will you do?"

He spread his arms in acceptance and resignation. He had no choice as to place of residence. His family had brought him here and installed him in the house; they gave him a tiny allowance but only on condition that he wouldn't return to Delhi. As was evident from his fluent English, Doctor Sahib was an educated man, though it was not quite clear whether he really had qualified as a doctor. If he had, he may have done something disreputable and been struck off the register.

30

Some such air hung about him. He was a great embarrassment to his family. Unable to make a living, he had gone around scrounging from family friends, and at one point had sat on the pavement in New Delhi's most fashionable shopping district and attempted to sell cigarettes and matches.

Later, when he had gone, Pritam said, "Don't you think I've got a dashing lover?"

"I know it's not true," the mother said, defending herself. "But other people, what will they think—alone with him in the house all winter? You know how people are."

"What people?"

It was true. There weren't any. To the mother, this was a cause for regret. She looked at the mountains stretching away into the distance—a scene of desolation. But Pritam's eyes were half shut with satisfaction as she gazed across the empty spaces and saw birds cleaving through the mist, afloat in the pure mountain sky.

"I was waiting for you all winter," the mother said. "I had your room ready, and every day we went in there to dust and change the flowers." She broke out. "Why didn't you come? Why stay in this place when you can be at home and lead a proper life like everybody else?"

Pritam laughed. "Oh but I'm not like everybody else! That's the last thing!"

The mother was silent. She could not deny that Pritam was different. When she was a girl, they had worried about her and yet they had also been proud of her. She had been a big, handsome girl with independent views. People admired her and thought it a fine thing that a girl could be so emancipated in India and lead a free life, just as in other places.

Now the mother decided to break her news. She said, "He

31

is coming with them on Thursday."

"Who is coming with them?"

"Sarla's husband." She did not look at Pritam after saying this.

After a moment's silence Pritam cried, "So let him come! They can all come—everyone welcome. My goodness, what's so special about him that you should make such a face? What's so special about any of them? They may come, they may eat, they may go away again, and goodbye. Why should I care for anyone? I don't care. And also you! You also may go—right now, this minute, if you like—and I will stand here and wave to you and laugh!"

In an attempt to stop her, the mother asked, "What will you cook for them on Thursday?"

That did bring her up short. For a moment she gazed at her mother wildly, as if she were mad herself or thought her mother mad. Then she said, "My God, do you ever think of anything except food?"

"I eat too much," the old lady gladly admitted. "Dr. Puri says I must reduce."

Pritam didn't sleep well that night. She felt hot, and tossed about heavily, and finally got up and turned on the light and wandered around the house in her nightclothes. Then she unlatched the door and let herself out. The night air was crisp, and it refreshed her at once. She loved being out in all this immense silence. Moonlight lay on top of the mountains, so that even those that were green looked as if they were covered in snow.

There was only one light—a very human little speck, in all that darkness. It came from Doctor Sahib's house, some way below hers. She wondered if he had fallen asleep with the light on. It happened sometimes that he dozed off where he was sitting and when he woke up again it was morning. But other times he really did stay awake all night, too excited by his reading and thinking to be able to sleep. Pritam decided to go down and investigate. The path was very steep, but she picked her way down, as sure and steady as a mountain goat. She peered in at his window. He was awake, sitting at his table with his head supported on his hand, and reading by the light of a kerosene lamp. His house had once had electricity, but after the disaster last winter it could not be got to work again. Pritam was quite glad about that, for the wiring had always been uncertain, and he had been in constant danger of being electrocuted.

She rapped on the glass to rouse him, then went round to let herself in by the door. At the sound of her knock, he had jumped to his feet; he was startled, and no less so when he discovered who his visitor was. He stared at her through his one glass lens, and his lower lip trembled in agitation.

She was irritated. "If you're so frightened, why don't you lock your door? You should lock it. Any kind of person can come in and do anything he wants." It struck her how much like a murder victim he looked. He was so small and weak—one blow on the head would do it. Some morning she would come down and find him lying huddled on the floor.

But there he was, alive, and, now that he had got over the shock, laughing and flustered and happy to see her. He fussed around and invited her to sit on his only chair, dusting the seat with his hand and drawing it out for her in so courtly a manner that she became instinctively graceful as she settled herself on it and pulled her nightdress over her knees.

"Look at me, in my nightie," she said, laughing. "I suppose you're shocked. If Mother knew. If she could see me!

33

But of course she is fast asleep and snoring in her bed. Why are you awake? Reading one of your stupid books—what stuff you cram into your head day and night. Anyone would go crazy."

Doctor Sahib was very fond of reading. He read mostly historical romances and was influenced and even inspired by them. He believed very strongly in past births, and these books helped him to learn about the historical eras through which he might have passed.

"A fascinating story," he said. "There is a married lady—a queen, as a matter of fact—who falls hopelessly in love with a monk."

"Goodness! Hopelessly?"

"You see, these monks—naturally—they were under a vow of chastity and that means—well—you know . . ."

"Of course I know."

"So there was great anguish on both sides. Because he also felt burning love for the lady and endured horrible penances in order to subdue himself. Would you like me to read to you? There are some sublime passages."

"What is the use? These are not things to read in books but to experience in life. Have you ever been hopelessly in love?"

He turned away his face, so that now only his cardboard lens was looking at her. However, it seemed not blank but full of expression.

She said, "There are people in the world whose feelings are much stronger than other people's. Of course they must suffer. If you are not satisfied only with eating and drinking but want something else . . . You should see my family. They care for nothing—only physical things, only enjoyment."

"Mine exactly the same."

"There is one cousin, Sarla—I have nothing against her,

34

she is not a bad person. But I tell you it would be just as well to be born an animal. Perhaps I shouldn't talk like this, but it's true."

"It is true. And in previous births these people really were animals."

"Do you think so?"

"Or some very low form of human being. But the queens and the really great people, they become—well, they become like you. Please don't laugh! I have told you before what you were in your last birth."

She went on laughing. "You've told me so many things," she said.

"All true. Because you have passed through many incarnations. And in each one you were a very outstanding personality, a highly developed soul, but each time you also had a difficult life, marked by sorrow and suffering."

Pritam had stopped laughing. She gazed sadly at the blank wall over his head.

"It is the fate of all highly developed souls," he said. "It is the price to be paid."

"I know." She fetched a sigh from her innermost being.

"I think a lot about this problem. Just tonight, before you came, I sat here reading my book. I'm not ashamed to admit that tears came streaming from my eyes, so that I couldn't go on reading, on account of not being able to see the print. Then I looked up and I asked, 'Oh, Lord, why must these good and noble souls endure such torment, while others, less good and noble, can enjoy themselves freely?'"

"Yes, why?" Pritam asked.

"I shall tell you. I shall explain." He was excited, inspired now. He looked at her fully, and even his cardboard lens seemed radiant. "Now, as I was reading about this monk—a

35

saint, by the way—and how he struggled and battled against nature, then I could not but think of my own self. Yes, I too, though not a saint, struggle and battle here alone in my small hut. I cry out in anguish, and the suffering endured is terrible but also—oh, Madam—glorious! A privilege.''

Pritam looked at a crack that ran right across the wall and seemed to be splitting it apart. One more heavy snowfall, she thought, and the whole hut would come down. Meanwhile he sat here and talked nonsense and she listened to him. She got up abruptly.

He cried, "I have talked too much! You are bored!''

"Look at the time," she said. The window was milk-white with dawn. She turned down the kerosene lamp and opened the door. Trees and mountains were floating in a pale mist, attempting to surface like swimmers through water. "Oh my God," she said, "it's time to get up. And I'm going to have such a day today, with all of them coming.''

"They are coming today?''

"Yes, and you needn't bother to visit. They are not your type at all. Not one bit.''

He laughed. "All right.''

"Not mine, either," she said, beginning the upward climb back to her house.

Pritam loved to cook and was very good at it. Her kitchen was a primitive little outbuilding in which she bustled about. Her hair fell into her face and stuck to her forehead; several times she tried to push it back with her elbow but only succeeded in leaving a black soot mark. When her mother pointed this out to her, she laughed and smeared at it and made it worse.

Her good humour carried her successfully over the arrival

36

of the relatives. They came in three carloads, and suddenly the house was full of fashionably dressed people with loud voices. Pritam came dashing out of the kitchen just as she was and embraced everyone indiscriminately, including Sarla and her husband, Bobby. In the bustle of arrival and the excitement of many people, the meeting went off easily. The mother was relieved. Pritam and Bobby hadn't met for eight years—in fact, not since Bobby had been married to Sarla.

Soon Pritam was serving a vast, superbly cooked meal. She went around piling their plates, urging them to take, take more, glad at seeing them enjoy her food. She still hadn't changed her clothes, and the smear of soot was still on her face. The mother—whose main fear had been that Pritam would be surly and difficult—was not relieved but upset by Pritam's good mood. She thought to herself, why should she be like that with them—what have they ever done for her that she should show them such affection and be like a servant to them? She even looked like their servant. The old lady's temper mounted, and when she saw Pritam piling rice onto Bobby's plate—when she saw her serving *him* like a servant, and the way he turned round to compliment her about the food, making Pritam proud and shy and pleased—then the mother could not bear any more. She went into the bedroom and lay down on the bed. She felt ill; her blood pressure had risen and all her pulses throbbed. She shut her eyes and tried to shut out the merry, sociable sounds coming from the next room.

After a while Pritam came in and said, "Why aren't you eating?"

The old lady didn't answer.

"What's the matter?"

"Go. Go away. Go to your guests."

37

"Oh my God, she is sulking!" Pritam said, and laughed out loud—not to annoy her mother but to rally her, the way she would a child. But the mother continued to lie there with her eyes shut.

Pritam said, "Should I get you some food?"

"I don't want it," the mother said. But suddenly she opened her eyes and sat up. She said, "You should give food to him. He also should be invited. Or perhaps you think he is not good enough for your guests?"

"Who?"

"Who. You know very well. You should know. You were with him the whole night."

Pritam gave a quick glance over her shoulder at the open door, then advanced toward her mother. "So you have been spying on me," she said. The mother shrank back. "You pretended to be asleep, and all the time you were spying on me."

"Not like that, Daughter—"

"And now you are having filthy thoughts about me."

"Not like that!"

"Yes, like that!"

Both were shouting. The conversation in the next room had died down. The mother whispered, "Shut the door," and Pritam did so.

Then the mother said in a gentle, loving voice, "I'm glad he is here with you. He is a good friend to you." She looked into Pritam's face, but it did not lighten, and she went on, "That is why I said he should be invited. When other friends come, we should not neglect our old friends who have stood by us in our hour of need."

Pritam snorted scornfully.

"And he would have enjoyed the food so much," the

38

mother said. "I think he doesn't often eat well."

Pritam laughed. "You should see what he eats!" she said. "But he is lucky to get even that. At least his family send him money now. Before he came here, do you want to hear what he did? He has told me himself. He used to go to the kitchens of the restaurants and beg for food. And they gave him scraps and he ate them—he has told me himself. He ate leftover scraps from other people's plates like a sweeper or a dog. And you want such a person to be my friend."

She turned away from her mother's startled, suffering face. She ran out of the room and out through the next room, past all the guests. She climbed up a path that ran from the back of her house to a little cleared plateau. She lay down in the grass, which was alive with insects; she was level with the tops of trees and with the birds that pecked and called from inside them. She often came here. She looked down at the view but didn't see it, it was so familiar to her. The only unusual sight was the three cars parked outside her house. A chauffeur was wiping a windscreen. Then someone came out of the house and, reaching inside a car door, emerged with a bottle. It was Bobby.

Pritam watched him, and when he was about to go back into the house, she aimed a pebble that fell at his feet. He looked up. He smiled. "Hi, there!" he called.

She beckoned him to climb up to her. He hesitated for a moment, looking at the bottle and toward the house, but then gave the toss of his head that she knew well, and began to pick his way along the path. She put her hand over her mouth to cover a laugh as she watched him crawl up toward her on all fours. When finally he arrived, he was out of breath and dishevelled, and there was a little blood on his hand where he had grazed it. He flung himself on the grass beside her and

39

gave a great "Whoof!" of relief.

She hadn't seen him for eight years, and her whole life had changed in the meantime, but it didn't seem to her that he had changed all that much. Perhaps he was a little heavier, but it suited him, made him look more manly than ever. He was lying face down on the grass, and she watched his shoulder-blades twitch inside his finely striped shirt as he breathed in exhaustion.

"You are in very poor condition," she said.

"Isn't it terrible?"

"Don't you play tennis any more?"

"Mostly golf now."

He sat up and put the bottle to his mouth and tilted back his head. She watched his throat moving as the liquid glided down. He finished with a sound of satisfaction and passed the bottle to her, and without wiping it she put her lips where his had been and drank. The whisky leaped up in her like fire. They had often sat like this together, passing a bottle of Scotch between them.

He seemed to be perfectly content to be there with her. He sat with his knees drawn up and let his eyes linger appreciatively over the view. It was the way she had often seen him look at attractive girls. "Nice," he said, as he had said on those occasions. She laughed, and then she too looked and tried to imagine how he was seeing it.

"A nice place," he said. "I like it. I wish I could live here."

"You!" She laughed again.

He made a serious face. "I love peace and solitude. You don't know me. I've changed a lot." He turned right round toward her, still very solemn, and for the first time she felt him gazing full into her face. She put up her hand and said quickly, "I've been cooking all day."

40

He looked away, as if wanting to spare her, and this delicacy hurt her more than anything. She said heavily, "I've changed."

"Oh no!" he said in haste. "You are just the same. As soon as I saw you, I thought: Look at Priti, she is just the same." And again he turned toward her to allow her to see his eyes, stretching them wide open for her benefit. It was a habit of his she knew well; he would always challenge the person to whom he was lying to read anything but complete honesty in his eyes.

She said, "You had better go. Everyone will wonder where you are."

"Let them." And when she shook her head, he said, in his wheedling voice, "Let me stay with you. It has been such a long time. Shall I tell you something? I was so excited yesterday thinking: Tomorrow I shall see her again. I couldn't sleep all night. No, really—it's true."

Of course she knew it wasn't. He slept like a bear; nothing could disturb that. The thought amused her, and her mouth corners twitched. Encouraged, he moved in closer. "I think about you very often," he said. "I remember so many things—you have no idea. All the discussions we had about our terrible social system. It was great."

Once they had had a very fine talk about free love. They had gone to a place they knew about, by a lake. At first they were quite frivolous, sitting on a ledge overlooking the lake, but as they got deeper into their conversation about free love (they both, it turned out, believed in it) they became more and more serious and, after that, very quiet, until in the end they had nothing more to say. Then they only sat there, and though it was very still and the water had nothing but tiny ripples on it, like wrinkles in silk, they felt as if they were in a

41

storm. But of course it was their hearts beating and their blood rushing. It was the most marvellous experience they had ever had in their whole lives. After that, they often returned there or went to other similar places that they found, and as soon as they were alone together that same storm broke out.

Now Bobby heaved a sigh. To make himself feel better, he took another drink from his bottle and then passed it to her. "It's funny," he said. "I have this fantastic social life. I meet such a lot of people, but there isn't one person I can talk with the way I talk with you. I mean, about serious subjects."

"And with Sarla?"

"Sarla is all right, but she isn't really interested in serious subjects. I don't think she ever thinks about them. But I do."

To prove it, he again assumed a very solemn expression and turned his face toward her, so that she could study it. How little he had changed!

"Give me another drink," she said, needing it.

He passed her the bottle. "People think I'm an extrovert type, and of course I do have to lead a very extrovert sort of life," he said. "And there is the business too—ever since Daddy had his stroke, I have to spend a lot of time in the office. But very often, you know what I like to do? Just lie on my bed and listen to nice tunes on my cassette. And then I have a lot of thoughts."

"What about?"

"Oh, all sorts of things. You would be surprised."

She was filled with sensations she had thought she would never have again. No doubt they were partly due to the whisky; she hadn't drunk in a long time. She thought he must be feeling the way she did; in the past they had always felt the same. She put out her hand to touch him—first his cheek, which was rough and manly, and then his neck, which was soft and smooth. He had been talking, but when she touched him he fell silent. She left her hand lying on his neck, loving to touch it. He remained silent, and there was something strange. For a moment, she didn't remove her hand—she was embarrassed to do so—and when at last she did she noticed that he looked at it. She looked at it too. The skin was rough and not too clean, and neither were her nails, and one of them was broken. She hid her hands behind her back.

Now he was talking again, and talking quite fast. "Honestly, Priti, I think you're really lucky to be living here," he said. "No one to bother you, no worries, and all this fantastic scenery." He turned his head again to admire it and made his eyes sparkle with appreciation. He also took a deep breath.

"And such marvellous air," he said. "No wonder you keep fit and healthy. Who lives there?" He pointed at Doctor Sahib's house below.

Pritam answered eagerly. "Oh, I'm very lucky—he is such an interesting personality. If only you could meet him."

"What a pity," Bobby said politely. Down below, there was a lot of activity around the three cars. Things were being rolled up and stowed away in preparation for departure.

"Yes, you don't meet such people every day. He is a doctor, not only of medicine but all sorts of other things too. He does a lot of research and thinking, and that is why he lives up here. Because it is so quiet."

Now people could be seen coming out of Pritam's house. They turned this way and that, looking up and calling Pritam's name.

"They are looking for you," Bobby said. He replaced the

43

cap of his whisky bottle and got up and waited for her to get up too. But she took her time.

"You see, for serious thinking you have to have absolute peace and quiet," she said. "I mean, if you are a real thinker, a sort of philosopher type."

She got up. She stood and looked down at the people searching and calling for her. "Whenever I wake up at night, I can see his light on. He is always with some book, studying, studying."

"Fantastic," Bobby said, though his attention was distracted by the people below.

"He knows all about past lives. He can tell you exactly what you were in all your previous births."

"Really?" Bobby said, turning toward her again.

"He has told me all about my incarnations."

"Really? Would he know about me too?"

"Perhaps. If you were an interesting personality. Yes all right, coming!" she called down at last.

She began the steep climb down, but it was so easy for her that she could look back at him over her shoulder and continue talking. "He is only interested in studying highly developed souls, so unless you were someone really quite special in a previous birth he wouldn't be able to tell you anything."

"What were you?" Bobby said. He had begun to follow her. Although the conversation was interesting to him, he could not concentrate on it, because he had to keep looking down at the path and place his feet with caution.

"I don't think I can tell you," she said, walking on ahead. "It is something you are supposed to know only in your innermost self."

"What?" he said, but just then he slipped, and it was all he

44

could do to save himself from falling.

"In your innermost self!" she repeated in a louder voice, though without looking back. Nimbly, she ran down the remainder of the path and was soon among the people who had been calling her.

They were relieved to see her. It seemed the old lady was being very troublesome. She refused to have her bag packed, refused to get into the car and be driven up to Simla. She said she wanted to stay with Pritam.

"So let her," Pritam said.

Her relatives exchanged exasperated glances. Some of the ladies were so tired of the whole thing that they had given up and sat on the steps of the veranda, fanning themselves. Others, more patient, explained to Pritam that it was all very well for her to say let her stay, but how was she going to look after her? The old lady needed so many things—a masseuse in the morning, a cup of Horlicks at eleven and another at three, and one never knew when the doctor would have to be called for her blood pressure. None of these facilities was available in Pritam's house, and they knew exactly what would happen—after a day, or at the most two, Pritam would send them an SOS, and they would have to come back all the way from Simla to fetch her away.

Pritam went into the bedroom, shutting the door behind her. The mother was lying on her bed, with her face to the wall. She didn't move or turn round or give any sign of life until Pritam said, "It's me." Then her mother said, "I'm not going with them."

Pritam said, "You will have to have a cold bath every day, because I'm not going to keep lighting the boiler for you. Do you know who has to chop the wood? Me, Pritam."

45

"I don't need hot water. If you don't need it, I don't."

"And there is no Horlicks."

"Tcha!" said her mother. She was still lying on the bed, though she had turned round now and was facing Pritam. She did not look very well. Her face seemed puffed and flushed.

"And your blood pressure?" Pritam asked.

"It is quite all right."

"Yes, and what if it isn't? There is no Dr. Puri here, or anyone like that."

The mother shut her eyes, as if it were a great effort. After a time, she found the strength to say, "There is a doctor."

"God help us!" Pritam said, and laughed out loud.

"He *is* a doctor." The mother compressed her little mouth stubbornly over her dentures. Pritam did not contradict her, though she was still laughing to herself. They were silent together but not in disagreement. Pritam opened the door to leave.

"Did you keep any food for him?" the mother said.

"There is enough to last him a week."

She went out and told the others that her mother was staying. She wouldn't listen to any arguments, and after a while they gave up. All they wanted was to get away as quickly as possible. They piled into their cars and waved at her from the windows. She waved back. When she was out of sight, they sank back against the car upholstery with sighs of relief. They felt it had gone off quite well this time. At least there had been no quarrel. They discussed her for a while and felt that she was improving; perhaps she was quietening down with middle age.

Pritam waited for the cars to reach the bend below and then—quite without malice but with excellent aim—she

46

threw three stones. Each one squarely hit the roof of a different car as they passed, one after the other. She could hear the sound faintly from up here. She thought how amazed they would be inside their cars, wondering what had hit them, and how they would crane out of the windows but not be able to see anything. They would decide that it was just some stones crumbling off the hillside—perhaps the beginning of a landslide; you never could tell in the mountains.

She picked up another stone and flung it all the way down at Doctor Sahib's corrugated tin roof. It landed with a terrific clatter, and he came running out. He looked straight up to where she was standing, and his one lens glittered at her in the sun.

She put her hands to her mouth and called, "Food!" He gave a sign of joyful assent and straightaway, as nimble as herself, began the familiar climb up.

# BOMBAY

Sometimes the Uncle did not visit his niece for several days. He stayed in his bare, unventilated lodging and fed himself with food from the bazaar. Once, after such an absence, there was a new servant in the niece's house, who refused to let him in. "Not at home!" the servant said, viewing the Uncle with the utmost suspicion. And indeed who could blame him; certainly not the Uncle himself.

But Nargis, the niece, the mistress of the house, was annoyed—not with the servant but with her uncle. In any case, she was usually annoyed with him when he reappeared after one of his absences. It was resentment partly at his having stayed away, partly at his having reappeared.

"Look at you," she said. "Like a beggar. And I suppose you have been eating that dirty bazaar food again. Or no food at all."

She rang the bell and gave orders to a servant, who soon returned with refreshments. The Uncle enjoyed them; sometimes he did enjoy things in that house, though only if he and she were alone together.

That could never be for long. Khorshed, one of her unmarried sisters-in-law, was soon with them, greeting the Uncle with the formal courtesy—a stately inclination of the head—that she extended to everyone. Since he was family, she also smiled at him. She had yellow teeth and was yellow all over; her skin was like thin old paper stretched over her bones. She sat in one of the winged armchairs by the window—her usual place, which enabled her to keep an eye on the road and anything that might be going on there. She entertained them with an account of a charity ball she had witnessed at the Taj Mahal Hotel the day before. Soon she was joined by her sister Pilla, who took the opposite armchair in order to see the other end of the road. They always shared a view between them in this way. They had done the same the day before at the Taj Mahal Hotel. They themselves had not bought tickets—it had not been one of their charities—but had taken up a vantage point on the velvet bench on the first landing of the double staircase. Khorshed had watched the people who had come up from the right-hand wing, and Pilla those from the left. Now they described who had been there, supplementing each other's account and sometimes arguing whether it had been Lady Ginwala who had worn a tussore silk or Mrs. Homy Jussawala. They quarrelled over it ever so gently.

Rusi came in much later. He had only just got up. He always got up very late; he couldn't sleep at night, and moved around the house and played his record-player at top volume. When he came in—in his brocade dressing-gown and with his hair tousled—everyone in the room became alert and intense, though they tried to hide it. His two aunts bade him good morning in sweet fluting voices; his mother inquired after his breakfast. He ignored them all. He sank into a chair, scowling heavily and supporting his forehand on his hand, as if weighted down by thoughts too lofty for anyone there to understand.

"Look, look," said Pilla to create a diversion, "here she is again!"

"Where!" cried Khorshed, helping her sister.

"There. In *another* new sari. Walking like a princess—and

49

they owe rent and bills everywhere."

"Just see—a new parasol too, matching the sari."

Both shook their heads. The boy, Rusi, took his hand from his brow, and his scowling eyes swept around the room and rested on the Uncle.

"Oh, back again," he said. "Thought we'd got rid of you." He gave one of his short, mad laughs.

"Yes," said the Uncle, "here you see me again. I had no food at home, so I came. Because of this," he said, patting his thin stomach.

"All dogs are like that," Rusi said. "Where there is food to be got, there they run. Have you heard of Pavlov? Of course not. You people are all so ignorant."

"Tell us, darling," said Nargis, his mother.

"Please teach us, Rusi darling," the aunts begged eagerly.

He relapsed into silence. He sat hunched in the chair and, drawing his feet out of his slippers, held them up one by one and studied them, wriggling the toes. He did this with great concentration, so that no one dared speak for fear of disturbing him.

The Uncle now forced himself to look at him. Every time he came here, it seemed to him that the boy had deteriorated further. Rusi had a shambling, flabby body, and though he was barely twenty his hair was beginning to fall out in handfuls. He was dreadful. The Uncle, instead of feeling sorry for this sick boy, hated him more than any other human being on earth. Rusi looked up. Their eyes met; the Uncle looked away. Rusi gave another of his laughs and said, "When Pavlov rang a bell, saliva came out of the dog's mouth." He tittered and pointed at the Uncle. "We don't even have to ring a bell! Khorshed, Pilla—look at him! Not even a bell!"

The women laughed with him, and so did the Uncle,

50

though only after he had caught his niece's eye and had read the imploring look there. Then it was not so difficult for him to join in; in fact, he wanted to.

Everyone always thought of the Uncle as a bachelor, but he had once been married. His wife had been dull and of a faded colour, and soon he sent her back to her parents and went to live with his brother and with Nargis, the brother's daughter. The brother's wife had also been dull and faded; she did not have to be sent away, but died, leaving the two brothers alone with the girl. These three had lived together very happily in a tiny house with a tiny garden that had three banana plants and a papaya tree in it. This was in an outlying suburb of Bombay, with a lot of respectable neighbours who did not quite know what to make of the household. It included an ancient woman servant, who was sometimes deaf, sometimes dumb, sometimes both. Whatever the truth of her disability, it prevented her from communicating with anyone outside the house and quite often with anyone in it. The two brothers didn't work much, though Nargis's father was a journalist and the Uncle a lawyer. They only went out to practise their respective professions when money ran very low. Then Nargis's father made the rounds of the newspaper offices, and the Uncle sat outside the courts to draw up documents and write legal letters. The rest of the time, they stayed at home and amused Nargis. They were both musical, and one sang while the other accompanied him on the harmonium. The whole household kept very odd hours, and sometimes when they got excited over their music they stayed up all night and slept through the day, keeping the shutters closed. Then the neighbours, wondering whether something un- toward had happened, stood outside the little house and

51

peered through the banana plants, until at last, toward evening, the shutters would be thrown open and a brother would appear at each window, fresh and rested and smiling at the little crowd gathered outside.

Both were passionate readers of Persian poetry and Victorian poetry and prose. They taught Nargis everything they could, and since she was in any case not a keen scholar, there was no necessity to send her to school. Altogether they kept her so much to themselves that no one realized she was growing up, till one day, there she was—a lush fruit, suddenly and perfectly ready. The two brothers carried on as if nothing had happened—singing, reading poetry, amusing her to the best of their ability. They bought her all sorts of nice clothes too, and whatever jewelry they could afford, so that it became necessary for them to go out to work rather more frequently than in the past. Nargis's father began to accept commissions to write biographies of prominent members of their own Parsi community. He wrote these in an ornate, fulsome style, heaping all the ringing superlatives he had gathered from his Victorian readings onto these shrewd traders in slippers and round hats. In this way, he was commissioned to write a biography of the founder of the great commercial house of Paniwala & Sons. The present head of the house took a keen interest in the project and helped with researches into the family archives. Once he got so excited over the discovery of a document that he had himself driven to the little house in the suburb. That was how he first saw Nargis, and how he kept coming back again even after the biography had been printed and distributed.

Nargis had no objections to marrying him. He wasn't really old—in his late thirties—though he was already perfectly bald, with his head and face the same pale yellow colour. His

hands were pale too, and plump like a woman's, with perfectly kept fingernails. He was a very kind man—very kind and
gentle—with a soft voice and soft ways. He wanted to do
everything for Nargis. She moved into the family mansion
with him and his two sisters and with his servants and the
treasures he had bought from antique dealers all over
Europe. Positions were found in the house of Paniwala for
Nargis's father and the Uncle, so that they no longer had to
go out in order to work but only to collect their cheques.
Everyone should have been happy, and no one was. The little
house in the suburb died the way a tree dies and all its leaves
drop off and the birds fly away. It was the old woman who felt
the blight first and had herself taken to hospital to die there.
Next, Nargis's father lay down with an ailment that soon
carried him off. Then the Uncle moved out of the house and
into his quarters in the city.

Nargis had once visited him there, to persuade him to
come and live in the family mansion. He wouldn't hear of it.
He also said, "Who asked you to come here?" He was quite
angry. Her arrival had thrown the whole house—indeed, the
whole neighbourhood—into commotion. A crowd gathered
around her large car parked outside, and some lay waiting on
the stairs, and children even opened the door of his room to
peep in at the grand lady who had come. He bared his teeth
at them and made blood-curdling noises.

"Come," Nargis pleaded. She looked round the room,
which was quite squalid, though it had a patterned marble
floor and coloured-glass panes set in a fan above the door.
The house had once been a respectable merchant's dwelling,
but now, like the whole neighbourhood, it was fast turning
into a slum.

53

"You needn't talk with anyone," she promised. "Only with me."

"And Khorshed?" he asked. "And Pilla?" He opened his mouth wide to laugh. He got great amusement out of the two sisters.

"Only with me."

He gave an imitation of Khorshed and Pilla looking out of the window. Then he laughed at his joke. He jumped up and cackled and hopped up and down on one foot with amusement.

"You haven't come for four days," she accused him, above this.

He pretended not to hear, and went on laughing and hopping.

"What's wrong? Why not?" she persisted. "Don't you want to see me?"

"How is Paniwala?"

"He says bring Uncle. Get the big room upstairs ready. Send a car for him."

"Oh go away," he said, his laughter suddenly gone. "Leave me alone."

She wouldn't. Usually complaisant, even phlegmatic, she became quite obstinate. She sat on his rickety string bed and folded her hands in her lap. She said if he wasn't coming, then she was staying. She wouldn't move till he had promised that, even if he wouldn't go and live in the house, he would visit there every day. Then at last she consented to be led back to her car. He went in front, clearing a way for her by poking his stick at all the sightseers.

He kept his promise for a while and went to the house every day. But he was always glad to come back home again. He walked up and down in the bazaar, looking at the stalls and

54

the people, and then he sat outside the sweetmeat seller's and had tea and milk sweets and read out of his little volume of Sufi poetry. Sometimes he was so stirred that he read out loud for the benefit of the other customers and passers-by, even though they couldn't understand Persian:

"When you lay me in my grave,
don't say, 'Farewell, farewell.'
For the grave is a screen hiding the
cheers and welcome of the
people of Paradise.
Which seed was cast but did not
sprout?
And why should it be otherwise for
the seed of man?
Which bucket went down but
came not up full of water?"

Then it seemed to him that everything had become suffused in purity and brightness—yes, even this bazaar where people haggled and made money and passed away their time in idle, worldly pursuits. He walked slowly home and up the wooden stairs, which were so dark (he often reproached the landlady) that one could fall and break one's neck. He went past the common lavatory and the door of the paralytic landlady, which was left open so that she could look out. He sat by the open window in his room, looking at the bright stars above and the bright street below, and couldn't sleep for hours because of feeling so good.

In the Paniwala house, it always seemed to be mealtime. A great deal of food was cooked. Paniwala himself could only eat very bland boiled food, on account of his weak digestion. Khorshed had a taste for Continental food masked in cheese sauces, while for Pilla a meal was not a meal if it was not rice

55

with various curries of fish and meat and a great number of spicy side dishes. Servants passed around the table with dishes catering to all these various tastes. The sideboard that ran the length of the wall carried more dishes under silver covers, and there were pyramids of fruits, bought fresh every morning, that were so polished and immaculate that they appeared artificial. The meals lasted for hours. Plates kept getting changed and everyone chewed very slowly, and it got hotter and hotter, so that the Uncle, eating all he could, felt as if he were in a fever. The sisters talked endlessly, but their conversation seemed an activity indistinguishable from masticating. By the time the meal was over, the Uncle felt his mind and body bathed in perspiration, and in this state he had to retire with them into the drawing-room, where sleep overtook everyone except Nargis and himself. The afternoon light that filtered through the slatted blinds made the room green and dim like an ocean bed; and uncle and niece sat staring at each other among the marble busts and potted plants, while the snores of the sleeping family lapped around them.

Once, as they sat like that, the Uncle saw tears oozing out of Nargis's eyes. It took him some time to realize they *were* tears—he stared at her as they dropped—and then he said in exasperation, "But what do you want?"

"Come and live here."

"No!" he cried like a drowning man.

All that had been a long time ago, before Rusi was born. After that event, although the Uncle continued to live in his slum house and the Paniwala family continued to eat their succession of meals, there was a change in both establishments. During one very heavy Bombay monsoon, an upper balcony of the Uncle's house collapsed and the whole tenement suffered a severe shock, so that the cracks on the staircase walls gaped wider and plaster fell in flakes from the ceilings. What remained of the coloured window-panes dropped out, and some were replaced with plain glass and some with cardboard and some were simply forgotten till more rain came. Also, in the same year as this heavy monsoon, the Uncle's skin began to discolour. This was not unexpected; leucoderma was a family disease and, indeed, very prevalent in the Parsi community. The Uncle first noticed the small telltale spot on his thumb. Of course, the affliction continued to spread and then the spots broke out all over him like mildew, so that within a few years he was completely discoloured. It was neither a painful nor a dangerous disease, only disfiguring.

The change in the Paniwala family was both more positive and more far-reaching. Somehow no one had expected any offspring, so that when Rusi nevertheless appeared, everyone was too excited to notice that his head was rather big or that it took him a long time to sit up. He was three before he could walk. "Let him take his time," they all said, and his slowness became a virtue, like the growth of a very special flower that one must wait upon to unfold. Only the Uncle did not much like to look at him. Rusi was always the centre around which the rest of the family was, quite literally, grouped. With his big head shaking, he tottered around on the carpet making guttural sounds, while they formed a smiling circle around him, encouraging him, calling his name, reciting long-forgotten baby rhymes, holding out loving fingers for him to steady himself on. They nodded at each other, and their soft, yellow, middle-aged faces beamed. And Nargis was one of them. The Uncle did not, as far as he could help it, look at the

57

child; he looked at her. She had changed. Motherhood had ripened and extended her, and she was almost fat. But it suited her, and her eyes, which had once been tender and misty and shining as if through a veil, were now luminous with fulfilment. They never looked at the Uncle—only at her son.

The Uncle tried staying away. At first he thought he liked it. He sat for hours outside the sweetmeat seller's and read and talked to everyone who had time. He also talked to the people who lived in the tenement with him—especially with the paralytic landlady. She had as much time as he did. She had spent over twenty years lying on her bed, looking out of the open door at the people going up and down on the stairs. Sometimes he went in and sat with her and listened to her reflections on the transient stream of humanity flowing past her door. She was a student of palmistry and astrology and was always keen to tell his fortune. She grasped his dis-coloured hand and studied it very earnestly and ignored his jokes about how the only fortune still left to him was the further fading of his pigmentation. She traced the lines of his palm and said she still saw a lot of beautiful living left. Then he turned the joke and said, "What about you?" Quite seriously, she stretched out her palm and interpreted its lines, and they too, it seemed, were as full of promise as a freshly sown field.

However long he stayed away now, Nargis never came to visit him or sent him any messages. If he wanted to see her, he had to present himself there. When he did, she rarely seemed pleased. His clothes were very shabby—he only possessed two shirts and two patched trousers, and never renewed them till they were past all wear—but whereas before Rusi's birth Nargis had taken his appearance entirely for granted, now she often asked him, "Why do you come like that? How

58

do you think it looks?" He feigned surprise and looked down at himself with an innocent expression. She was not amused. Once she even lost her temper and shouted at him that if he did not have enough money to buy clothes, then please take it from her; she said she would be glad to give it to him. Of course, he did have enough, as she knew; his cheques came in regularly. Suddenly she became more angry and pulled out some rupee notes and flung them at his feet, and rushed out of the room. There was a moment's silence; everyone was surprised, for she was usually so calm. Then one of the sisters bent down to pick up the money, gently clicking her tongue as she did so.

"She is upset," she said.

"Yes, because of Rusi," said the other sister.

"He had a little tummy trouble last night."

"Naturally, she is upset."

"Naturally."

"A mother . . ."

"Of course."

They went on like that, like a purling, soothing stream. They did this partly to cover up for Nargis, and partly for him, so that he might have time to collect himself. Although he sat quite still and with his gaze lowered to the carpet, he was trembling from head to foot. After a time, ignoring the sisters, he got up to leave. He walked very slowly down the stairs and was about to let himself out when Nargis called to him. He looked up. She was leaning over the curved banister with Rusi, whom she was dancing up and down in her arms. "Ask Uncle to come up and play with us!" she told Rusi. "Say, 'Please, Uncle! Please, Uncle dear!'" For reply, Rusi opened his mouth wide and screamed. The Uncle did not look up again but continued his way toward the front door, which a servant was holding open for him. Nargis called down loudly, "Where are you going!"

At that the child was beside himself. His face went purple and his mouth was stretched open as wide as it would go, but no screams came out. This made him more frantic, and he caught his fingers in his mother's hair, pulling it out of its pins, and then flailed his hands against her breasts. He was only three years old but as strong as a demon. She fell to the floor, with him on top of her. The Uncle ran up the stairs as fast as he could. He tried to help her up, tugging at her from under the child, who now began to flail his fists at the Uncle.

"Yes yes, I'm all right," Nargis said, to reassure them both. She managed to sit up; her hair was about her shoulders and there were scratches on her face. "Where are you going?" she asked the Uncle.

"I'm not going," he said. "I'm here. Can't you see?" he shouted, "I'm here! Here!" very loudly, in order to make himself heard above the child's screams.

As Rusi grew up, it was decided that he was too brilliant. He did too much thinking. His mother and aunts were disturbed to see him sitting scowling and hunched in an armchair, sunk in deep processes of thought. Occasionally he would emerge with some fragment dredged up from that profundity. "There will be a series of natural disasters due to the explosion of hitherto undiscovered minerals from under the earth's surface," he might say. He would fix his aunts with his brooding eyes and say, "You look out." Then they became very disturbed—not because of his prophecy but because they feared the damage so much mental activity might do his brain. They would try and bring him some distraction—share some exciting piece of news with him

60

regarding a wedding or a tea party, or feed him some sweet thing that he liked. Sometimes he accepted their offering graciously, sometimes not. He was unpredictable, though very passionate in his likes and dislikes.

The person to whom Rusi took the deepest dislike was the Uncle. He baited him mercilessly and had all sorts of unpleasant names for him. The one he used most frequently was the Leper, on account of the Uncle's skin disease. Sometimes he said he could not bear to be in the house with him and that either the Uncle or he himself must leave. Then the Uncle would leave. Next time he came, Rusi might be quite friendly to him—it was impossible to tell. The Uncle tried not to mind either way, and the rest of the family did all they could to make it up to him. At least Paniwala and his sisters did; Nargis was more unpredictable. Sometimes, when Rusi had been very harsh, she would follow the Uncle to the door and be very nice to him, but other times she would encourage Rusi and clap her hands and laugh loudly in applause and then jeer when the Uncle got up to go away. On such occasions, the Uncle did not take the train or bus but walked all the way home through the city in the hope of tiring himself out. He never did, though, but lay awake half the night, saying to himself over and over, "Now enough, now enough." Then he thought of the landlady downstairs eagerly reading in his palm that great things were still in store for him. It made him laugh, for he was in his seventies now.

Rusi ordered a lot of books, though he did not do much reading. His aunts said he didn't have to, because he had it all in his head already. For the same reason, there was not much point in his going to school; he only quarrelled with the teachers, who were very ignorant and not at all up to his standards. In all the schools he tried, everyone eventually agreed

61

that it would be better for him to leave. Then came a succession of private tutors, but here too there was the same trouble—there was just no one who knew as much as he did. Those who did not leave quite soon of their own accord had to be told to go, because their inferior qualities made him take such a dislike to them. Once he got so angry with one of them that he stabbed him with a penknife. Although everyone was disturbed by this incident, still no one said anything beyond what they always said: the boy was too highly strung. It came, his aunts explained, from having too active a mind. They recommended more protein in his diet and some supplementary vitamin pills. Nargis listened to them eagerly and went out to buy the pills. The three women tried to coax him to take them, but he laughed in derision and told them how he had a method, evolved by himself, of storing extra energy in his body through his own mineral deposits. He had plans to patent this method and expected to make a large fortune out of it. The aunts shook their heads behind his back and tapped their foreheads to indicate that he had too much brilliance for his own good. When he looked at them, they changed their expression, to appear as interested and intelligent as possible. He said that they were a couple of foolish old women who understood nothing, so what was the use of talking to them; the only person in the house who might understand something of what he was saying was his father, who was going to put up the money for the project.

His father was not seen very much in the house nowadays. It seemed he was very busy in the office and spent almost all his time there. Weeks passed when the Uncle did not meet him at all. When he did, he found him more gentle than ever, but there was something furtive about him now and he did not like to meet anyone's eye. If he was present while Rusi was baiting the Uncle, he tried to remonstrate. He said, "Rusi, Rusi," but so softly that his son probably failed to hear him. After a while, he would get up and quietly leave the room and not come back. Once, though, when this happened, the Uncle found him waiting for him downstairs by the door. "One moment," Paniwala said and drew him into his study; he pressed the Uncle's hand as he did so. The Uncle wondered what he was going to say, and he waited and Paniwala also waited. A gold clock could be heard ticking in a very refined way.

When Paniwala at last did speak, it was on an unexpected subject. He informed the Uncle that the oil painting on the wall above his desk—it was of the Paniwala ancestor who had founded their fortune—was not done from life but had been copied from a photograph. Even the photograph was the only one of him known to be in existence; he had not been a man who could be induced to pose very often in a photographer's studio.

"He came to Bombay from a village near Surat," Paniwala said. "To the end of his days, what he relished most was the simple village food of chapati and pickle. He built this house with many bathrooms, but still he liked to take his bath in a bucket out in the garden, thereby also watering the plants."

Paniwala chuckled, and both of them looked up at the portrait, which showed a shrivelled face with a big bony Parsi nose sticking out of it. Paniwala also had a big nose, but his was not bony; it was soft and fleshy. Altogether he looked very different from his ancestor, being very much softer and gentler in the contours of his face and in expression.

"He was a very strict man," Paniwala said. "With himself and also with others. Everyone had to work hard, no slacking

63

allowed. My grandfather also got this discipline from him. Yes, in those days they were different men—a different breed of men." He passed his hands over his totally bald head. When he spoke again, it was to say, "Your expenses must have gone up; money is not what it was. I wonder if your cheque . . . You'll excuse me." He lowered his eyes.

The Uncle waved his hand in a gesture that could mean anything.

"You'll allow me," said Paniwala, terribly ashamed. "From the first of next month. Thank you. The little house where he was born, near Surat, is still there. It is so small you would not believe that the whole family lived there. There were nine children, and all grew up healthy and well. Later he brought his brothers and brothers-in-law to Bombay, and everyone did well and they too had large families . . . You are going? No, you must take one of the cars—what are they all standing there for? Allow me." But the Uncle wanted to walk, so Paniwala escorted him to the door. He told him how his grandfather had always insisted on walking to the warehouse, even when he was very old and quite unsteady, so that the family had made arrangements for a carriage and an attendant to follow him secretly.

The two sisters also often spoke about their family—not about past generations but about the present one. They were always visiting relatives, many of whom were bedridden, and then they would come home and discuss the case. Sometimes they predicted an early end, but this rarely came to pass. The family tended to be very long-lived, and though crippled by a variety of diseases, the invalids lingered on for years and years. They stayed in their mahogany bedsteads and were fed and washed by servants. There was also an imbecile call-ed Poor Falli, who had lived in the same Edwardian house for

64

over fifty years, though confined to one room with bars on the windows; he was not dangerous, but his personal habits made it difficult for other people. The two sisters spoke about all these family matters quite openly now before the Uncle. It had not always been so. True, they had always been scrupulously polite to him—ignoring his shabby clothes, calling him by his first name, never omitting a greeting to him on entering or leaving a room—but he had remained an outsider. Nor had they forgotten the difference between his family and theirs. But as the years passed they regarded him more and more as one of themselves. This happened not all at once, but gradually, and only after Rusi's birth—an event, in the eyes of the sisters, that had finally drawn the two families together and made them as one.

The Uncle fell ill with fever. He lay in his room, tossing on his string bed, which had no sheets but only a cotton mat and a little pillow hard as a stone. Neighbours came in and, because he was shivering so much, covered him with a blanket and tried to make him drink milk and soup. He let them do whatever was necessary. His body felt as if it were been broken up bone by bone by someone wielding a stone hammer. He wondered whether he was going to die now. All the time he was smiling—not outwardly, for he groaned and cried out so much that the neighbours were very worried and sent messages to the Paniwala house, but inside himself. Sometimes he thought he was at the sweetmeat seller's, sometimes he saw himself back in the little house in the suburb with his brother and the old woman and Nargis ripening like a fruit in sunshine. It didn't matter in which of these places he fancied himself, for they were both wonderful, a foretaste of Paradise. He thought if he were really going to die

65

now, he would never need to return to the Paniwala house at all. When he thought of this, tears welled into his eyes and flowed down his cheeks, so that the neighbours exclaimed in pity.

When Nargis came, he was better. The fever had abated and he lay exhausted. He had not died and yet he felt dead, as if everything were spent. Nargis wasted no time. She paid what was left of his rent and reimbursed the neighbours. They helped her pack up his things. He kept wanting to say no, but he didn't have the strength. Instead he wept again; only now the tears were cold and hard. The neighbours, not seeing the difference, told Nargis that he had been weeping like that all through his sickness, and when she heard this, she also wept. At last he was carried down the stairs, and as they passed the door of the paralytic landlady, she called out to him in triumph, "You see! It has come true what I said! It was all written in your hand."

Sometimes, as he lay in the large fourposter in the Paniwala bedroom, he looked at his hand and wondered which were the lines that had told the landlady about the new life awaiting him. It was very still and quiet in that room. He gazed at the painting on the opposite wall; it had been specially commissioned and showed a scene in the Paniwala counting house at the beginning of the century. The Paniwala founder sat at a desk high up on a dais, and his sons at other desks on a slightly lower dais, and they overlooked a hall full of clerks sitting crosslegged in rows and writing in ledgers. It had been done in dark, murky colours, to look like a Renaissance painting. When he was tired of it, he looked at the other wall, where there was a window and the top of a tree just showing against it. Nargis had engaged a servant for

66

him, who made his bed and washed him and performed other personal functions. Khorshed and Pilla came in at least once a day and sat on either side of him and told him everything that was happening, in the family and in Bombay society in general. Rusi also came in; he had been warned to be good to his uncle, and for quite some time he observed this injunction. But as the weeks and then the months passed and the Uncle still lay there, Rusi could not help himself and reverted to his former manner. He was especially gleeful if he happened to come in while the Uncle was being fed. This had to be done very carefully and with a specially curved spoon, and even then quite a lot went to waste and trickled down the Uncle's chin.

It was usually his servant who fed the Uncle, but sometimes Nargis did it herself. Although she was less satisfactory than the servant and got impatient quite quickly, the Uncle much preferred her to do it. Then he would linger over his food as long as possible. Then Rusi could stand there and say what he liked—the Uncle didn't care at all. He just looked into Nargis's face. She always sat with her back to the window and the tree. Even when she got annoyed with him—saying, "You are doing it on purpose," when the food dropped on his chin—still he loved to have her sitting there. At such times it seemed to him that his landlady had been right and that his life was not over by any means.

# ON BAIL

Although I get tired working in the shop all day, once I reach home I forget all about it. I change into an old cotton sari and tuck it round my waist and I sing as I cook. Sometimes he is at home but not often, and usually only if he is sick with a cold. What a fuss he makes then; I have to take his temperature many times and prepare hot drinks and crush pills in honey and altogether feel very sorry for him. That's the best time, especially since he forgets quite soon about being sick and wants to amuse himself and me. How we laugh then, what a fine time we have! He doesn't seem to miss his friends and coffee houses and all those places one bit but is as happy to be at home with me as I am to be with him. Next evening, of course, he is off again, but I don't mind, for I know it's necessary—not only because he is a very sociable person but because it is for business contacts too.

I'm used to waiting up for him quite late, so I was not worried that night at all. When my cooking was finished, I sat at the table waiting for him. I love these hours; it is silent and peaceful and the clock ticks and I have many pleasant thoughts. I know that soon I will hear his step on the stairs, and the door will open and he will be there. I smile to myself, sitting there at the table with my head supported on my hand, full of drowsy thoughts. Sometimes I nod off and those thoughts turn into dreams on the same subject. But I always start up at the sound of his steps—only *his* steps, because that night Daddy was already in the room, calling my name,

68

before I woke up. Then I jumped to my feet. I knew something terrible had happened.

When Daddy said that Rajee had been arrested, I sank down again onto my chair. I couldn't stand, I couldn't speak. Daddy thought it was with shock, but of course it was out of relief. I had imagined far worse. It took me some time to realize that this too was very bad. I knew Daddy thought it was the worst thing there could be. He was so badly affected that I had to make him lie down while I prepared tea for him. I also served him the meal I had cooked for Rajee and myself. Daddy ate both our portions. Now that he is old, he seems to need a great deal of food and is always ready to eat at any hour, whatever his state of mind may be.

But when he had finished this time, he became very upset again. He pushed away the dish and said, "Yes, yes, yes, I knew how it would be."

Of course, this was no time to start defending Rajee. In any case, I have long stopped doing so. I know it isn't so much Rajee that Daddy doesn't like but the fact that I'm married to him and have not become any of the grand things Daddy wanted.

"A case of cheating and impersonation," Daddy said now. "A criminal case."

I cried, "But where is he?"

"In jail! In prison! Jail!"

Daddy moaned, and so did I. I thought of Rajee sitting in a cell. I could see him sitting there and the expression on his face. I put my head down on the table and sobbed. I could not stop.

After a while Daddy began to pat my back. He didn't know what else to do; unlike Rajee, he has never been good at comforting people. I wiped my eyes and said as steadily as I could, "What about bail?"

That made Daddy excited again; he cried, "Five thousand rupees! Where should we take it from?"

No, we didn't have five thousand rupees. Daddy only had his pension, and Rajee and I only had my salary from the shop. Again I saw Rajee sitting there, but I quickly shut my eyes against this unbearable vision.

I made Daddy comfortable on our bed and told him I would be back soon. He wanted to know where I was going. He asked how I could go alone in the streets at this time of night, but he was too tired to protest much. I think he was already asleep when I left. I had to walk all the way through the empty streets. I wasn't frightened, although there had lately been some bad cases in the newspapers of women being attacked. I had other things to think about, and chief among them at the moment was how I could wake up Sudha without waking the rest of her household. But this turned out to be no problem at all, because it was she who came to the door as soon as I knocked. I think she hadn't gone to sleep yet, although it was two o'clock in the morning. No one else stirred in the house.

When I told her, she had a dreadful shock. I think she had the same vision of him that I had. I put out my hand to touch her, but she pushed me away. The expression of pain on her face turned to one of anger. She said, "Why do you come here? What should I do?" Of course she knew what it was I wanted. She said, "I haven't got it." Then she shouted, "Do you know how long I haven't seen him! How many days!"

I looked around nervously, and she laughed. She said, "Don't worry. He wouldn't wake up if the house fell down." She was right; I could hear her husband snoring, with those fat sounds fat people make in their sleep. "Listen," she said.

"It's the same every night. He eats his meal and then—" She imitated the snoring sounds. "And I can't sleep. I walk round the house, thinking. Does Rajee talk about me to you? What does he say?"

I didn't know what to answer. I had already suspected that Rajee did not like to be with her as much as before, but I didn't want to hurt her feelings. Also, this was not the time to talk about it. I had to have the money from her. I had to. There was no other way.

When I said nothing, her face became hard. She and I have known each other for a long time—we were at college together—but I have always been a bit afraid of her. She is a very passionate person. "Go!" she said to me now, and her voice was hard. "How dare you come here? Aren't you ashamed."

"Where else can I go?"

We were silent. Her husband snored.

I said, "I had cooked fish curry for him tonight, he loves it so much. Do you think they gave him anything to eat there? You know how particular he is about his food."

She shrugged, like someone to whom this is of no concern. But I knew these were not her true feelings, so I continued. "Will he be able to sleep? I don't know if they give beds. Perhaps there are other people with him in the cell—bad characters. I've heard there are many people who share each cell, there is such overcrowding nowadays. And there are no facilities for them, only one bucket, and they take away their belts and shoelaces, because they are afraid that—"

"Be quiet!"

She went out of the room, stumbling over a footstool in her hurry. I could hear her in the bedroom, rattling keys and banging drawers. She took absolutely no care about making

71

a noise, but the sounds from her husband went on undisturbed. I waited for her. I didn't like being here. The room was furnished with costly things, but they were not in good taste. I have always disliked coming here. The atmosphere is not good, probably because she and her husband don't like each other.

At last she came back. She didn't have cash, but she gave me some jewelry. She had wrapped it in a cloth, which she thrust into my hands. Then she said, "Go, go, go," but that was not necessary, for I was already on my way out.

Rajee came home the next evening. I wished we could have been alone, but Daddy and Sudha were also there. Rajee smiled at them, but they both averted their eyes from him and then his smile faded. He didn't know what to say. Neither did I.

Rajee is so good-humoured and sociable that he hates it when the atmosphere is like that, and he feels he has to do something to cheer everyone up again. He rubbed his hands and said, "Nice to be home," in a cheerful, smiling voice.

Sudha shot him a burning look. Her eyes are already large enough, but they look even larger because of the kohl with which she outlines them.

"North, South, East, West, home is best," Rajee said.

"Fool! Idiot!" Sudha screamed.

There was a silence, in which we seemed to be listening to the echo of this scream. Then Rajee said, "Please let me explain."

"What is there to explain?" Daddy said. "Cheating, impersonation—"

"A mistake," Rajee said.

They were silent in a rather grim way, as if waiting to hear

72

what he had to say. He cleared his throat a few times and spread his hands and began a long story. It was very involved and got more and more so as he went on. It was all about some man he had met in the coffee house who had seemed an honest, decent person but had turned out not to be so. It was he who had drawn Rajee into this deal, which also had turned out not to be as honest and decent as Rajee had thought. I didn't listen very carefully; I was watching the two others to see what impression he was making on them. Rajee too was watching them, and every now and again he stopped to scan their faces, and then he ran his tongue over his lips and went on talking faster. He didn't once look at me, though; he knew it didn't make any difference to me what he said, because I was on his side anyway.

Rajee is a very good talker, and I could see that Sudha and Daddy were wavering. But of course they weren't happy yet, and they continued to sit there with very glum faces. So then Rajee, sincerely anxious to cheer them up, said to me, "How about some tea? And a few biscuits, if you have any?" He smiled and winked at me, and I also smiled and went away to make the tea.

When I came back, Daddy was arguing with Rajee. Daddy was saying, "But is this the way to do business? In a coffeehouse, with strangers, is this the way to make a living?" Rajee was proving to him that it was. He told him all big deals were made that way. He gave him a lot of examples of fortunes that had been made just by two or three people meeting by chance—how apartment houses had been bought and sold, and a new sugar mill set up with all imported machinery by special government license. It was all a matter of luck and skill and being there at the right time. I knew all these stories, for Rajee had told them to me many

73

times. He loves telling them and thinking about them; they are his inspiration in life. It is because of them, I think, that he gets up in such good humour every day and hums to himself while shaving and dresses up smartly and goes out with a shining, smiling face.

But Daddy remained glum. It is not in his nature to believe such stories. He is retired now, but all through his working life he never got up in good humour or ever went to his office with high expectations. All he ever expected was his salary, and afterward his pension, and that is all he ever got.

"Do you know about Verma Electricals, how they started—have you any idea?" Rajee said, flushed with excitement. But Daddy said, "It would be better to get some regular job."

Rajee smiled politely. He could have pointed out—only he didn't, because he is always very careful of people's feelings—that the entire salary that Daddy had earned throughout his thirty-five years of government service was less than Rajee can expect to make out of one of his deals.

Now Daddy started to get excited. His lips trembled and his hands fumbled about in the air. He said, "If you—Then she—she—she—" He pointed at me with a shaking finger. We all knew what he meant. If Rajee got a job, then I wouldn't have to go to work in the shop.

I said, "I like it."

Daddy got more excited. He stammered and his hands waved frantically in the air as if they were searching for the words that wouldn't come to him. Rajee tried to soothe him. He kept saying, "Please, Daddy." He was afraid for his heart.

And, indeed, Daddy's hands suddenly left off fumbling in the air and clutched his side instead. He must have got one of

74

his tremors. He started whimpering like a child. Rajee jumped up and kept saying, "Oh my goodness." He took Daddy's arm to lead him to our sofa and make him lie down there. Rajee said several times, "Now keep quite calm," but in fact it was he who was the most excited.

I got Daddy's pills and Sudha got water and Rajee ran for pillows. Daddy lay on the sofa, with his eyes shut. He looked quite exhausted, as if he didn't want to say or think anything more. Rajee kept fussing over him, but after a time there was nothing more to be done. Daddy was all right and fast asleep. Rajee said to me, "Sit with him." I took a cane stool and sat by the sofa holding Daddy's hand.

But I wasn't thinking of him, I was watching the other two. There was going to be a big scene between them, I knew. Rajee also knew it, and he was very uncomfortable. Sudha lounged in a chair in the middle of the room, with her legs stretched out before her under her sari. She was wearing a brilliant emerald silk sari and gold-and-diamond earrings. She seemed too large and too splendid for our little room. Everything in the room appeared very shabby—the old black oilcloth sofa with the white cotton stuffing bulging out where the material has split; the rickety little table with the cane unwinding like apple peel from the legs; last year's free calendar hanging from a nail on the wall, which hasn't been whitewashed for a long time. I only notice these things when she is here. She makes everything look shabby—me included. Only Rajee matches up to her. Even now, after a night in jail, he looked plump and prosperous and he shone, the way she did.

He was waiting for her to say something, but she only looked at him from under her big lids, half lowered over her big eyes. It seemed she was waiting for him to speak first. He

75

started telling her about Daddy's heart—about the attack last year and how careful we have had to be since then and how we always keep his pills handy. Suddenly she interrupted him. She did this in a strange way—by clutching the top part of her sari and pulling it down from her breasts. She commanded, "Look!"

What was he to look at? At her big breasts that swelled from out of her low-cut blouse? Modestly—because of Daddy and me being in the room—he lowered his eyes, but she repeated, "Look, look," in an impatient voice. She struck her hand against her bared throat.

"Your necklace," he murmured uncomfortably.

She threw a savage look in my direction, so that I felt I had to defend myself. I said to Rajee, "Where else could I get it from? Five thousand!"

He shook his head, as if rebuking me. This infuriated her, and she began to shout at me. She cried, "Yes, you should have left him there in jail where he belongs!"

"Sh-h-h, sh-h-h," said Rajee, afraid she might wake up Daddy.

She lowered her voice but went on with the same fury. "It's the place where you belong. Because you are not only a cheat but a thief also. Can you deny it? Try. Say, 'No, I'm not a thief.' No? Then what about that time in my house?" She turned to me. "I never told you, but now I will show you what sort of a person you are married to."

I didn't look at her but stared straight in front of me.

"I'll make him tell you himself. Tell her!" she ordered him, but the next moment she was shouting, "The servant caught him! He called me, 'Quick, quick, come quick, Memsahib,' and when I went into the room, yes, there he was with his hand right inside my purse. Oh, how he looked then! I

76

will never, never, never forget as long as I live his face at that moment!" She flung her hands before her face like someone who didn't want to see.

"I don't believe you," I said.

"Ask him!"

"I don't believe you."

Our clock ticked. It is a round battered old metal clock, and it ticks with a loud metal sound. Usually, when I am alone here sitting quietly at the table waiting for him, I like that sound; it is soothing and homely to me. But now, in the silence that had fallen between us, it was like a sick heart beating.

When Sudha spoke again, it was in quite a different voice. "It doesn't matter," she said. "I don't care at all." Then she said, "Whatever you need, you think I wouldn't give? Would I ever say no to you? If you want, take these too. Here—" She put up her hands to her earrings. "No, take them. Take," she said as he held out his hand to restrain her, though she did not go any farther in unhooking them. "That's all nothing. I don't care one jot. I only care that you haven't come. For so long you haven't come to me. Every Tuesday afternoon, every Thursday, I got ready for you and I waited and waited—Why are you looking at her!" she cried, for Rajee had glanced nervously in my direction. "Who is she to grudge me those few hours with you, when she has taken everything else!"

She got up from where she had been sprawled in the chair. I didn't know what she was going to do. She looked capable of anything; the room seemed too small for all she seemed capable of doing. I think Rajee felt the same, and that is why he took her away.

We have one more room besides this one, but we have to

cross an open passage to get to it. This is a nuisance during the rains, when sometimes we have to use an umbrella to go from our bedroom to our sitting room. We run across the passage under the umbrella, holding each other close. Now he was taking Sudha through our passage. I heard him shut the door and draw the big metal bolt from inside.

I was left alone with Daddy, who was sleeping with his mouth dropped open. He looked an old, old man. The clock ticked, loud as a hammer. I tried not to think of Rajee and Sudha in our bedroom, just as I always tried not to think of them in her house on Tuesday and Thursday afternoons (the days her husband goes to visit his factory at Saharanpur). Sometimes it is not good to think too much. Why dwell on things that can't be helped? Or on those that are over and done with? That is why I also don't look back on the past very much. There was a time when I didn't know Rajee but Sudha did. Of course she often spoke to me about him—I was her best friend—but I didn't meet him till I had to start taking letters between them. That was the time her family was arranging her marriage, and she and Rajee were planning to elope together. Well, it all turned out differently, so what is the use of thinking back now to what was then?

Daddy woke up. He looked round the room and asked where the other two were. I said Sudha had gone home and Rajee was sleeping in the bedroom because he was very tired after last night. Daddy groaned at the mention of last night. He said, "Do you know what it could mean? Seven years rigorous imprisonment."

"No, no, Daddy," I said. I wasn't a bit frightened; I didn't believe it for a moment.

"You may look in the penal code. Cheating and im-

78

personation, Section 420."

"It was all a mistake, Daddy. While you were sleeping, he explained everything to me."

I didn't want to hear anything more, and there was only one way I knew to keep him quiet. Although I couldn't find anything except one rather soft banana, he was glad to have even that. I watched him peeling it and chewing slowly, mulling it round in his mouth to make the most of every bite. Whenever I watch him eat nowadays, I feel he is not going to live much longer. I feel the same when I see him looking at the leaves moving on a tree. He enjoys these things like a person for whom they are not going to be there much longer.

He said, "How will you stay alone for seven years?"

I said, "No, Daddy."

I was saying no, it wouldn't happen, Rajee wouldn't be away for seven years, and also I was saying no, Daddy, I won't be alone, you won't die.

But he went on. "Yes, alone. You will be alone. I won't be here."

He turned away his face from me. I strained my ears towards the bedroom. But of course it was too far away, with the passage in between, to hear anything.

Daddy said, "These government regulations are very unfair. If there is a widow, the pension is paid to her, but otherwise it stops. Often I think if I had saved, but how was it possible? With high rent and college fees and other expenses?"

Daddy used to spend a lot of money on me. He sent me to the best school and college, where girls from much richer families went. He also tried to buy me the same sort of clothes that those girls had, so that I should not feel inferior to them.

I said, "I'm all right. I have my job."

79

"Your job!"

Daddy has always hated it that I work as cashier in a shop. Of course, from his point of view, and after all that expense and education, it isn't very much, but it is enough for Rajee and me to live on.

"They wanted a graduate. I couldn't have got it if I weren't a graduate." I said this to make him feel better and show him his efforts had not been wasted. "And sometimes there are some quite difficult calculations, so it's good I did all that maths at college."

"For this?" Daddy said, making the grubbing movement of counting coins with which he always refers to my job.

"Never mind," I said. "It doesn't matter."

Whenever we speak about this subject, we end up in the same way. Daddy used to have very high hopes for me. There were only the two of us, because my mother had died when I was born and Daddy didn't care for the rest of the family and had broken off relations with them. He cared only for me. He was proud because I did well at school and always stood first in arithmetic and English composition. At that time he used to read a lot. It's funny: nowadays he doesn't read at all; you would think in his retirement he would be reading all the time, but he doesn't—not even the newspaper. But at that time he was particularly fond of reading H. G. Wells and Bernard Shaw, and was keen for me to become like the women in their books. He said there was no need for me to get married; he said why should I be like the common run of girls. No, I must be free and independent and the equal of men in everything. He wanted me to smoke cigarettes, and even began to smoke himself so as to encourage me. (I didn't like the taste, so we both stopped.)

Now he said, "If he has to go, it would be better to give up this place and stay somewhere as paying guest."

"He doesn't have to go!"

"Or perhaps you can stay with a friend. What about her? What is her name?"

"Sudha? You want me to go and stay with her?"

I laughed and laughed; only at some point I stopped. I don't know if he noticed the difference. He may not have, because I was sitting on the floor with my knees drawn up and my face buried in them. All he would be able to see was my shoulders shaking, and that could be laughing *or* crying.

But I think he wasn't taking much notice of me. I think he was more interested in his own thoughts. He has a lot of thoughts always; I can tell because I can see him sunk into them and mumbling to himself and sometimes mumbling out loud. Perhaps that's the reason he doesn't read any more. I looked at him; he was shaking his head and smiling to himself. Well, at least he was thinking something pleasant that made him happy.

And I could think only of Sudha and Rajee in there in our bedroom! You would have said—anyone would have said—that I had the right to go and bang on the door and shout, "What are you doing! Come out of there!" I should have done it.

Daddy said, "The time I liked best was the exams. I watched you go in with the others and I knew you would do better than any of them. I was sure of it."

He chuckled to himself in the triumphant way he used to when the results came out and I had done well. He had always accompanied me right up to the door of the examination hall, and as I went in he shouted after me, "Remember! First Class first!" flexing the muscles of his arm as if to give me strength. It used to be rather em-

81

barrassing—everyone stared—and I hurried in, pretending not to be the person addressed. But I was glad to see him when I came out again and he was standing there waiting, always with some special thing he knew I liked, such as a bag of chili chips.

He had stopped chuckling. Now his face was sad. He turned up his hand and held it out empty. "In the end, what is there?" he said. "Nothing. Ashes."

Well, I couldn't sit there listening to such depressing talk! I jumped up. I went straight through the passage, and now I did bang on the door. The bolt was drawn back and Rajee opened the door. He said, "One minute. She is going now."

I said, "I told Daddy she has gone home."

Rajee understood the problem at once. We have only one entrance door, and to get to that Sudha would have to pass through the sitting room and walk past Daddy. He would be surprised to see her back again.

Rajee told me to wait till he called. He went into the sitting room. I heard him talk to Daddy in a loud, cheerful voice. I went into the bedroom. Sudha was buttoning up her blouse. She didn't take much notice of me but only glanced at me over her shoulder and went on straightening her sari and fixing her hair. She did not look happy or satisfied; on the contrary, her eyes and cheeks were swollen with tears, and I think she was still crying, without making any sound.

At last Rajee called. Sudha and I walked through the passage and into the sitting room. I made her walk on the far side of Daddy, along the wall, and Rajee had also got between us and Daddy to shield us from view. He was stirring something in a cup. "Just wait till you taste this, Daddy," he was saying. "It is called Rajee's Special. Once tasted, never forgotten." Daddy's attention was all on this cup, and he had even stretched out his hands for it. Sudha walked along the wall with her sari pulled over her head, not looking right or left. I think she was still crying. I took her as far as the stairs and I said, "Be careful," because there was no light on the stairs. She managed to grope her way down, though I didn't wait to see. I was in a hurry to get back into the room.

I said, "Daddy had better go home now, before it gets too late."

"How can he go?" Rajee said. "He is not well; he must stay here with us."

Suddenly I became terribly angry with Rajee. Perhaps I had been angry all the time—only now it came out. I began to shout at him. I shouted about the disgrace of getting arrested, but it wasn't only that; in fact, that was the least of it. Once I get angry, I find it very difficult to stop. New thoughts keep coming up, making me more angry, and I feel shaken through and through. I said many things I didn't mean.

Daddy joined in from time to time, saying what a disgrace it was to the family. The worse things I said the better pleased he was. When I showed signs of running down, he encouraged me to start up again. He listened attentively with his head to one side, so as not to miss anything, and whenever he thought I had scored a good point he thrust his forefinger up into the air and shouted, "Right! Correct!" He had become quite bright and perky again.

But Rajee sat there hunched together and with his head bowed, letting me say whatever I wanted, even when I called him a cheat and a liar and a thief. He sat there quiet and looking guilty. Then I wished that he would speak and rouse himself and perhaps get angry in return. I stopped every time

83

I had said something very bad, so that he might defend himself. But it was always Daddy who spoke. "Right," he said. "Correct," till at last I cried, "Oh, please be quiet, Daddy!"

"No," Rajee said. "He is right. I deserve everything you say, all the names you are calling me, for having worried you so much."

"Worried me about what?"

Rajee looked up in surprise. He made a vague gesture, as if too ashamed to mention what had happened.

"About what?"

Rajee lowered his eyes again.

"Oh, you think that's all," I said. "That you have been in jail. You think that's the worst thing you have done. Ha."

He looked quite blank. The idiot! Did he think that was nothing—to have been in our bedroom alone with Sudha? Was it so small a thing? Then I longed to do more than only shout at him. I longed really to strike and beat him. If only Daddy would go away!

Daddy said, "I'm very tired. I will stay here tonight."

"Yes, yes, quite right." Rajee jumped up. He got sheets and pillows and made up Daddy's bed on the sofa. Afterwards he turned down the sheet like a professional nurse and helped Daddy undress and arranged him comfortably. He spent rather a long time on all this, and appeared quite engrossed in it. I realized he was putting off being alone with me.

But I could wait. Soon Daddy would be asleep and then we would be alone. He would not be able to get away from me. I crossed the passage into our bedroom. I looked round carefully. It was as usual. There seemed to be no trace of Sudha left. It is strange; she has a very strong smell—partly

84

because she is heavy and perspires heavily and partly because of the strong perfumes she wears—but though I sniffed and sniffed the air, I found that nothing of her remained.

I stepped up close to the mirror to look at myself. I often do it—not so much because I'm interested in myself but because of a desire to check up on how I look to Rajee. I haven't changed much from the time he first knew me. I think small, skinny girls like me don't change as fast as big ones like Sudha. If it weren't for my long hair, I still could be taken either for a boy or a girl. When I was a child, people had difficulty in telling which I was because Daddy always had my hair cut short. He had a theory that it was a woman's long hair that was to blame for her lack of freedom. But later, when I grew bigger, I envied the other girls their thick, long hair, in which they wore ornaments and flowers, and I would no longer allow mine to be cut. It never grew very thick, though. Sometimes I try to wear a flower, but my hair is too thin to hold it and the flower droops and looks odd, so that sooner or later I snatch it out and throw it away.

Rajee called to ask if I wanted tea. I called back no. I realized he only wanted to put off the moment for us to be alone together. I felt angry and grim. But when he did come I stopped feeling like that. He stood in the door, trying to scan my face to see my mood. He tried to smile at me. He looked terribly tired, with rings under his eyes.

"Lie down," I said. "Go to sleep now." My voice shook, I had such deep feeling for him at that moment.

He was very much relieved that I had stopped being angry. He flung himself on the bed like a person truly exhausted. I squatted on the bed beside him and rubbed my fingers to and fro in his soft hair. He had his eyes shut and looked at peace.

After a time, I whispered, "Was it very bad?"

Without opening his eyes, he answered, "Only at first. Don't stop. I like it." I went on rubbing my fingers in his hair. "At first of course it was a shock, though everyone was quite polite. They allowed me to take a taxi, and two policemen accompanied me."

"They didn't—?" I asked. I had been thinking about this all the time, and it made me shudder more than anything. So often in the streets I had seen people led away to jail, and their wrists were handcuffed and they were fastened to a policeman with a long chain.

"Oh no," he said. He knew what I meant at once. "They could see they were dealing with a gentleman. The policemen were very respectful to me, and they accepted cigarettes from me and smoked them in the taxi, though they were on duty. And when we got there everyone was quite nice. They were quite apologetic that this had to be done." He opened his eyes and said, "I wish you hadn't taken the money from Sudha."

"Then from where?" I cried.

"Yes, I know. But I wish—"

"Should I have left you there?"

"No no, of course not." He spoke quickly, as if afraid that I would get angry again. And to prevent this from happening he pulled me down beside him and pressed me close and held me.

He seemed eager to tell me about the jail. He always likes to tell me everything, and I sit up for him at night and try and keep awake, however late he comes, because I know he is coming home with a lot to tell. Every day something exciting happens to him, and he loves to repeat it to me in every detail. Well, it seemed that even in jail he had had a good time, and it wasn't at all like what I had thought.

86

"You see," he explained, "before trial we are kept quite separate and we are allowed all sorts of facilities. It's really more like a hotel. Of course, there are guards, but they don't bother you at all. On the contrary, if they see you are a better-class person they like to help you. I met some very interesting people there—really some quite topnotch people; you'd be surprised."

I *was* surprised. I had no idea it could be like that. But that is one of the wonderful things about Rajee—wherever he goes, whatever he does, something good and exciting happens to him.

"As a matter of fact," he said, "I made a very good contact. Something interesting could come of it. Wait, I'll tell you."

I knew he wanted his cigarettes—he always likes to smoke when he has something nice to tell—so I got out of bed and brought them for him. He lit up, and we lay again side by side on the bed.

"There was this person in the patent-medicine line, who had been in for several days. It took time to arrange for his bail, because it was for a very big amount. There is a big case against him. Everyone—all the guards and everyone—was very respectful to him, and he was good to them too. He knew how to handle them. His food and other things came from outside, and he also had cases of beer and always saw to it that the guards had their share. Naturally, they did everything they could to oblige him. And they were very careful with me too, because they could see he had taken a great liking to me."

That was nothing new. Wherever he goes, people take a great liking to Rajee and do all sorts of things for him and want to keep him in their company.

"He insisted I should eat with him, though as a matter of

87

fact I wasn't very hungry, I was still rather upset. But the food was so delicious—such wonderful kebabs, I wish you could have tasted them. And plenty of beer with it, and plenty of good company, because there were some other people too, all in for various things but all of them better-class. We were quite a select group. Afterward we had a game of cards, that was good fun. Why are you laughing?"

It was all so different from what I had thought! I was laughing at myself, for my fears and terrible visions. I asked, "Did you win anything?"

"No, as a matter of fact I lost, but as I didn't have the money to pay they said it didn't matter, I could pay some other time."

"How much?" I asked, suddenly suspicious.

"Oh, not very much."

But he seemed anxious to change the subject, which confirmed my suspicions. My mood was no longer so good now. I began to brood. Here I had been, and Daddy and Sudha, and there he had been all the time, quite enjoying himself and even losing money at cards.

I said, "If it was so nice, perhaps I should have left you there."

He gave me a reproachful look and was silent for a while. But then he said, "I wish it had been possible to get the money from someone else."

"Why?" I said, and then I felt worse. "Why?" I repeated. "She is such a wonderful friend to you. So wonderful," I cried, "that you bring her here and lock yourself into our bedroom with her to do God knows what!"

He turned to me and comforted me. He explained everything. I began to see that he had had no alternative—that he *had* to bring her in here because of the way

88

she felt and because of the money she had given. He didn't say so outright, but I realized it was partly my fault also, for taking the money from her.

I felt much better. He went on talking about Sudha, and I liked it, the way he spoke about her. He said, "She is not a generous person; that is why it is not good to take from her. At heart, she grudges giving—it eats her up."

"She was always like that," I said, giving him a swift sideways look. But he agreed with me; he nodded. I saw that his feelings for her had completely changed.

"Every little bit she gives," he said, "she wants four times as much in return."

"It's her nature."

I remembered what she had said about his taking money from her purse. I felt indignant. To shame him like that, before her servant! Obviously, he would never have taken the money if he had not been in great need. She should have been glad to help him out. I never hide my money from him now. I used to sometimes—I used to put away absolutely necessary amounts, like for the rent—but he always seemed to find out my hiding places, so I don't do it anymore. Now if we run short I borrow it from the cash register in the shop; no one ever notices, and I always put it back when I get my salary. Only once I couldn't put it back—there were some unexpected expenses—but they never found out, so it's all right.

"What's that?" he said. We were both silent, listening. He said, "I think Daddy is calling."

"I don't hear anything."

Rajee wanted to go and see, but I assured him it was all right. Daddy might have called out in his sleep—he often did that. I asked Rajee to tell me more about his adventures last night, so he settled back and lit another cigarette.

89

"You know, this person I was telling you about—in the patent-medicine line? He wants me to contact him as soon as he comes out. He says he will put some good things in my way. He was very keen to meet me again and wanted to have my telephone number. . . . You know, it is very difficult without a telephone; it is the biggest handicap in my career. It is not even necessary to have an office, but a telephone—you can't do big business without one. Do you know that some of the most important deals are concluded over the telephone only? I could tell you some wonderful stories."

"I know," I said. He had already told me some wonderful stories on this subject, and I knew how much he longed for and needed a telephone, but where could I get it from?

"Never mind," he said. He didn't want me to feel bad. "When we move into a better place, we shall install all these things. Telephone, refrigerator—I think he *is* calling."

Rajee went to see. I also got off the bed and looked under it for my slippers. As I did so, I remembered a terrible dream I used to have as a child. I used to dream Daddy was dead. Then I screamed and screamed, and when I woke up Daddy was holding me and I had my arms round his neck. Afterwards I was always afraid to go on sleeping by myself and got into his bed. But I would never tell him my dream. I was frightened to speak it out.

When I came into the sitting room, I found Daddy sitting up on the sofa, and Rajee was holding him up under the arms—sort of propping him up. It was that time of the night when everything looks dim and depressing. We have only one light bulb, and it looked very feeble and even ghostly and did not shed much light. Dawn wasn't far off—it was no longer

90

quite night and it was not yet day—and the light coming in through the window was rather dreary. Perhaps it was because of this that Daddy's face looked so strange; he lay limp and lolling in Rajee's arms.

And he was very cross. He said he had been shouting for hours and no one came. In the end, he had had to get up himself and get his pills and the water to swallow them with. If it hadn't been for that—if he hadn't somehow got the strength together—then who knew what state we might have found him in later when we woke up from our deep sleep? Rajee kept apologizing, trying to soothe him, but that only seemed to make him more cross. He went on and on.

"Yes," he said, "and if something happens to me now, then what about her?" He pointed at me in an accusing way.

"Nothing will happen, Daddy," Rajee said, soothing him. "You are all right."

Daddy snorted with contempt. "Feel this," he said, guiding Rajee's hand to his heart.

"You are all right," Rajee repeated.

Daddy made another contemptuous sound and pushed Rajee's hand away. "You would have made a fine doctor. And who is going to look after her when you go? What will she do all alone for seven years?"

"He is *not going*, Daddy," I said, spacing my words very distinctly. I didn't like it, that he should still be thinking about that.

"Not going where?" Rajee asked.

That made Daddy so angry that he became quite energetic. He stopped lolling in Rajee's arms and began to abuse him, calling him the same sort of names I had called him earlier. And Rajee listened to him as he had listened to me, respectfully, with his head lowered.

91

I tried to bear it quietly for a while but couldn't. Then I interrupted Daddy. I said, "It is not like that at all."

"No?" he said. "To go to jail is not like that? Perhaps it's a nice thing. Perhaps we should say, 'Well done, Son. Bravo.'"

"He wasn't in jail," I said. "It was more like a hotel. And he met some very fine people there. You don't understand anything about these things, Daddy, so it's better not to talk."

Daddy was quiet. I didn't look at him, I was too annoyed with him. He had no right to meddle in things he didn't know about; he was old now, and should just eat and sleep.

"Lie down," I told him. "Go to sleep."

"All right," Daddy said in a meek voice.

But in fact he couldn't lie down, because Rajee had dropped off to sleep on the sofa. He was sitting up, but his head had dropped to his chest and his eyes were shut. Naturally, after two sleepless nights. I couldn't disturb him, so I told Daddy he had better go and sleep in our bedroom. Daddy said all right again, in the same meek voice. He carried his pillow under his arm and went away.

I lifted Rajee's legs onto the sofa and arranged his head. He didn't wake up. I looked at him sleeping. I thought that even if he had to go away for a while he would be coming back to me. And even if it were for a longer time there are always remissions for good conduct and other concessions, and meanwhile visits are allowed and I could take him things and also receive letters from him. So even if it is for longer, I shall wait and not do anything to myself. I would never do anything to myself now, never. I wouldn't think of it.

I did try it once. I got the idea from two people. One of them was Rajee. It was the time when Sudha's marriage was being arranged, and he came daily to our house and cried

92

and said he could not bear it and would kill himself. I think he felt better with being able to talk to me, but after I told him my feelings for him he didn't come so often anymore, and after a time he stopped coming altogether. Then I began to remember all he had said about what was the use of living. It so happened that just at this time there was a girl in the neighbourhood who committed suicide—not for love but because of cruel treatment from her in-laws. She did it in the usual way, by pouring kerosene over her clothes and setting herself on fire. It is a crude method and perhaps not suitable for a college girl like me, but it was the only way I could think of and also the easiest and cheapest, so I decided on it.

Only that day, when everything was ready, Daddy came home early and found me. Although he never wanted me to get married, he saw then that there was no other way and he sent for Rajee. When Daddy saw that Rajee was reluctant to get married to me, he did a strange thing—the sort of thing he has never, never in his whole life done to anyone. He got down on the floor and touched Rajee's feet and begged him to marry me. Rajee, who is always very respectful to elders, was shocked, and he bent down to raise him and cried, "Daddy, what are you doing!" As soon as I heard him say Daddy, I knew it would be all right. I mean, he wouldn't call him Daddy, would he, unless he was going to be his son-in-law?

# PROSTITUTES

Tara's house was in a newly developed area on the outskirts of town. It had been one of the first houses there, but in the last few years others had been coming up and tenants had moved into them. Tara didn't know any of these people and had no interest in making their acquaintance. She had got used to being on her own. She did not even miss her daughter, Leila; indeed, in many ways it was a relief not to have her there.

Leila's father, Mukand Sahib, came every day—often twice a day. He too was relieved to have Leila away at boarding school, for in recent years the girl had taken a dislike to him. It had been a difficult situation, and the cause of half the fights between mother and daughter. The other half had been due to the presence of Bikki, although, unlike Mukand Sahib, Bikki had not at all minded the girl's tantrums. On the contrary, he seemed to enjoy teasing her into them. Bikki did not increase his visits when Leila was sent away. In fact, nowadays Tara saw nowhere near enough of him. Sometimes, hearing some noise at the door, she thought he had come and hurried out to meet him. But it was usually only Mukand Sahib. Then she found it difficult to curb her irritation.

Mukand Sahib did everything he could to placate her. He had become very humble with her, which irritated her more than ever. She watched him sitting in her living room one hot summer day, panting with heat and not even daring to ask

94

her for a glass of water. She did not offer him one. She was too angry and disappointed with him for not being Bikki. She sat with her face averted, though she was aware of his imploring looks. He was wiping his forehead with his handkerchief. He appeared to be really suffering, but all he said was "It is very hot outside."

It was as if she had been waiting for this. "Then why come here?" she cried. "I'm sure your wife will be very happy to keep you at home! Why come and sit on my head?"

When he did not reply, she glanced at him out of the corner of her eye. He was trembling, and he looked terribly old. She began to be nervous. What if he were to have a stroke here and now, in her house? She realized she would have to be more careful. She forced herself to say, "Should the servant bring water for you?" He nodded, unable to speak, though his eyes now gazed at her in gratitude.

She shouted for the servant, but he did not come. She went to the door and shouted in a voice so loud that the thin little house seemed to shake. Still he did not come; he was a new servant and very unreliable. Soon she would have to change him (she often changed her servant). She went out to the water jug and filled a glass for Mukand Sahib. He drank it off at once, and she went to get another. When she came back with that, he seized her hand and kissed it.

Although she overcame her desire to snatch her hand away, she felt she could not stay with him a moment longer. Mumbling that she was going to make tea for him, she swiftly left the room. She went up on the roof. It was intensely hot there, with the sun beating down in a white hot glare, but she felt it was the only place where she could breathe. She found it difficult to draw in sufficient breath. She laid her hand on her breasts—large and still firm, though she was nearing

95

forty—and took great gulps of air. The spot on her hand where his lips had been felt like a sore, and she wiped it again and again on her sari. She sank down by the parapet and buried her head in her knees. She did not know what to do. She did not think she could ever go back into that house, back into the room where he was waiting for her to return. Yet it was unbearable on the roof; the bricks burned like fire. All around the landscape was arid, as desolate as a desert, and the new houses scattered over it, some of them half finished, looked like skeletons picked bare and bleached in the sun.

When Mukand Sahib had first bought this house for her, almost ten years ago, she had been very happy to live in it. She had not felt lonely at all, although at that time there had been only one other building nearby (a contractor's office, since abandoned). She had eaten and slept and played with Leila, and in the evenings she had dressed herself up to wait for Mukand Sahib. Quite often he had not been able to come. He had been busy in those years—not only with his law practice and his family obligations but also with his various honorary positions, such as vice-president of the local Rotary Club. She had been very proud of him and of his attachment to her and of everything he did for her and their daughter. No other woman in her family had ever been so well settled—not her mother or her grandmother or anyone else. Of course, they had all had admirers in their youth, and had borne children to them, and had even been kept by them for a while, but none of them had been taken out of her surroundings and provided for and kept in a good position, the way she had been by Mukand Sahib.

He was calling her now; she could hear his plaintive, old man's voice from the house below. She wiped the tears and perspiration from her face and after a while managed to pull

96

herself together sufficiently to go down to him. He was sitting in the same place she had left him, on the mattress in one corner. When she came in, he said, "Why do you leave me? Don't leave me." He didn't ask about the tea she had promised him. He only wanted her to be there, as near to him as possible. "Here," he pleaded, feebly patting the mattress. Again overcoming herself, she approached him, sat by him. He laid his hand in her lap and sighed with contentment. "Don't leave me," he said again.

"Why should I leave you?" she said in the gruff way in which she usually spoke to him nowadays. "Where should I go? I was right here, in the kitchen." Then, cunningly, taking advantage of his contentment, she said, "But today I have to go and visit my mother." When she saw the pain and disappointment on his face, she shouted, "I have to! Don't you understand!"

"Yes yes, I understand," he said quickly.

"My God, how selfish you are. Naturally, Maji wants to see me. She is lonely, now that he has gone." Her mother's companion—an old man who had been with her for many years—had recently died.

"You think you are the only person who needs me," Tara went on. "You have no thought for anyone but yourself. That is the sort of person you are—I have always known it."

There was a silence. Then he said, "You should take a little present for your mother."

"All right."

"Please take it from my pocket."

She put her hand in and drew out his money and counted it. She kept all of it except for one rupee, which she put back. The rest she folded and thrust down into her bosom—but with rather a stern air, as if she were doing him a favour. And

97

he really seemed to feel it was a favour, for he took up the hand with which she had taken the money and kissed it again. This time she was quite complaisant about it. Poor old man, she thought—though absently, for she was already looking forward to the expedition to her mother's house.

Her mother still lived in the Quarter, just behind the street of the silversmiths. She was the oldest tenant in her building, and everyone knew her and called her Maji. The other tenants were all much younger women who still practised their profession, and the house was always ringing with the noise of musical instruments and ankle bells. At night there was a lot of coming and going; men chewing betel felt their way up the dark stairs, and quite often there were brawls. Music came from the mother's room too, for she still liked to entertain herself with singing. Now, however, all her songs were devotional. Sometimes the other tenants came in to listen to her—they sighed and looked thoughtful—but she didn't care if anyone was there or not; she sang anyway. She was singing when Tara arrived, and though she smiled and nodded at her daughter, she didn't stop till the song had ended. She was accompanying herself on the harmonium. It was strange seeing her do that, because in the past the old man, her companion, had always been there to play for her.

The last time Tara had been in this room had been the day the old man had died. His corpse had lain there on a plank, covered with red cloth up to the chin. His face was exposed, not looking much different from when he was alive. The room was crowded, mostly with the other tenants. They were crying bitterly, although they had all disliked him. He used to lurk on the stairs, waiting for them in order to start quarrelling over some trifle. Of course all that was forgotten

98

now that he was a corpse draped with marigolds. Loud wailing broke out when the plank was lifted up, to be carried downstairs and through the streets on its way to the burning ground. All the women rushed to the top of the stairs for a last look. Maji, of course, wailed the loudest and had to be supported under both arms while she beat her breasts and struck her head against the wall.

But now, two weeks later, she was singing and smiling and really just the same as ever. The room too was the same—the most comfortable place Tara knew on earth. It was crowded with objects: musical instruments, brass vessels, a hookah, a birdcage, a faded folding screen with a hole in the silk. It was also fragrant with incense and scented betel. Tara stretched herself out on the mattress on the floor in an attitude of complete relaxation. Her large limbs were sprawled in all directions. She could never relax like that in her own house.

As soon as Maji had finished her song, Tara asked, "Has Bikki been here?"

"Yes. And the child? Has a letter come? What does she say? Are they giving sufficient food in the school?"

Maji was passionately fond of Leila, her only grandchild, and did not seem to mind at all that Leila hardly ever came to see her, or that when she did she was very surly with her.

When Tara had given all the news of Leila, she asked again about Bikki. Again Maji's reply was brief and evasive. Tara asked many more questions: When had he come? How long had he stayed? Was he so busy that he had no time to visit Tara?

When Maji found it impossible to be evasive any longer, she made excuses for Bikki. Yes, she said, he had been busy, but it was for her sake, for Maji. He had been very kind to her and had done some of the little errands for her that the old man used to do. Tara became calmer and was even able to think of her mother instead of Bikki. "It must be difficult for you," she said. "After so many years."

Maji and the old man had been together from before the time when Tara was born. He was not Tara's father—that had been someone else, long since vanished—but he had served Maji in many capacities; as musician, pimp, errand boy, lover when there had been no one else and she had still needed someone. In his last years he had done whatever small services he could in return for being allowed to live here with Maji and eat her food.

Maji said, "He was old. And I'm old, too. Perhaps it will be my turn next." She cackled rather gleefully, as if this were a treat to be looked forward to.

Tara snapped her fingers in the air several times, to keep ill luck away. "Will he come today?" she asked.

"Who?"

"Bikki."

Maji changed the subject. "And Mukand Sahib?" she asked. She murmured a blessing upon the air, as was her habit when speaking of her daughter's benefactor.

"He sent this for you." Tara fumbled in her bosom for the money.

"Where was the need?" protested Maji, quickly tucking it into her own bodice.

"Do you know where Bikki is? Can you send for him?" Tara was no longer relaxed on the mattress but straining forward to hear her mother's reply.

At last Maji said, "Leave it."

Tara sank back onto the mattress. She lay there like a sick woman. "I *have* to see him," she said, with such anguish that Maji realized there was no help for it.

100

Bikki came very quickly—too quickly—but Tara was so relieved to see him that she did not start thinking about that. In any case, Bikki did not give her much time to think. He came into the room with his usual bounce and high spirits, ready to charm and please. Soon he had them all in a festive mood. He was so gallant with Maji that she simpered and turned aside to hide her face behind her hand in a gesture of coquetry that sprang fresh from her youth. As for Tara, all the pain of longing and separation was forgotten, as the pangs of childbirth are forgotten in the moment of delivery. Her face was radiant; her eyes were only on him. She feasted on him. He was a rather stocky, broad-shouldered young man, with a round face blooming with smiles, sparkling black eyes, and glossy black hair that nestled low on the nape of his neck. He was dressed very beautifully, as always, in wide white freshly starched muslin and embroidered slippers. Tara took his hand in hers and turned his ring around and around on the little finger on which he wore it. She had bought that ring for him with money that Mukand Sahib had given her to pay a dentist's bill. She kissed the ring, and then he kissed it, and then they smiled at each other and their eyes spoke.

Suddenly Bikki jumped up and said, "Listen!" He squatted on the floor by the harmonium and began to play a new tune and sing the words to it. He didn't know it very well, but he had quite a sweet voice and sang with so much pleasure that they had to like it too. He broke off in the middle and cried, "It is wonderful, wonderful! Oh! '*Didn't you hear my heart cry out as you plucked it.*' Oh, oh!" He threw himself down on the floor and rolled around there while clutching his heart, like one suffering excruciating pain. The two women laughed, and he was satisfied and sat up, smiling to have given pleasure.

101

He said to Tara, "Now it is your turn. Make us happy with a beautiful song sung in your own beautiful voice."

"Get away!" She pretended to hit him. Tara was quite unmusical. Her mother and grandmother had worked hard to train her, but whenever she had begun to sing they covered their ears with their hands. Actually, it had not mattered. Tara in her heyday had brought more professional engagements into the family than they had ever had before. When men saw her, they forgot about singing and dancing and were content just to look.

Maji said, "But our little Leila, our angel, she has the true gift."

Tara shrugged. It was true that Leila seemed to have inherited her grandmother's voice rather than her mother's looks. But she had never cared to learn the family tradition of singing; she hated it above everything.

"Ah, when is she coming?" cried Bikki. "I miss our little Missie Sahib so much."

"You are very cruel to her," Tara said.

"No, it is she who is cruel to me." He rubbed his forehead ruefully. During her last holidays, she had thrown a cup at him. It had broken, and a piece had cut him and he had bled. Leila had run into the bedroom and locked the door. Then Tara ran about, alternately sponging Bikki's head and pounding on the door to get Leila to come out. But Leila did not emerge till late in the evening, after Bikki had left. Her face was swollen and she refused to speak to Tara for several days afterward—in fact, not until it was time to return to school and Tara took her to the railway station.

Now Bikki decided that he was hungry. He told them of a new place he had discovered, not far away at all, where excellent meat pilao was to be had. He would go and get some

102

for the three of them straightaway, and some carrot halwa as well. He waited tactfully for Tara to give him money, and the way he took it was very tactful too, his palm closing over it in a delicate, unobtrusive manner. He was already running down the stairs when Tara called him back; he stopped and looked up at her, and she ran down to meet him and threw her arms around his neck on the dark stairs. She wouldn't let go of him, though he tried to disengage himself. "Someone will come," he whispered. He looked up apprehensively, but she didn't care at all. She was stroking his neck and discovered a thin gold chain around it. Surprised, she drew it out to look at it. "Who gave this to you?" she asked. Then he managed to free himself and ran as quickly as he could down the stairs.

Tara returned to her mother in a pensive mood. All sorts of suspicions now arose in her mind. She brooded while Maji played the harmonium and softly sang to herself. At last Tara said, "Where was he when you sent for him?" She had recollected how quickly Bikki had appeared; he must have been somewhere in the building to appear so quickly. What was he doing there? And with whom? These thoughts were like thorns.

"*Where?*" she shouted.

Maji stopped playing. The last note hung on the air, together with Tara's shout.

"Upstairs," Maji answered at last.

"Who with? Tell me. . . . No, you must." Tara was struggling to speak calmly, and struggling also to keep herself together. She suffered from high blood pressure, and in moments of agitation her heart thumped as if it wanted to burst through her body.

103

Maji said, "What does it matter? What is it to you?"
Although Tara made a feeble gesture, asking her to stop saying such things, Maji went on bravely. "You can wait for
seven births and plead and pray with folded hands, and still
you will not meet again a person like Mukand Sahib," she
said. She repeated her customary blessing on him.

Tara managed to prop herself on her elbow. "Who is he
with? Which one?" she said. "Is it Salima?" Maji did not
reply, and Tara sank back and said, "I thought so."

Salima was a women who had moved into the house a few
months before. She was rather charming and had quite a few
customers. She could well afford to keep Bikki and give him
gold chains. She may have been a few years older than Bikki,
but of course she was still many years younger than Tara.

Now Tara was cursing Bikki and Salima both. She swore
what she would do to them—hack their bones into tiny
pieces, pluck out their eyes to feed to vultures. She acted out
how she would do these dreadful things. Maji tried to calm
her. She shouted above Tara's shouts, she held Tara's arms,
which were flailing in the air. It was as if she were struggling
with devils that possessed her daughter.

Tara was exhausted. She lay still and allowed Maji to
brush away the strands of hair that clung with perspiration
to her forehead. Maji murmured endearments. She also kept
repeating the name and virtues of Mukand Sahib, as if he
were some kind of balm that she was applying to her
daughter's hurt.

But Tara said, "I don't want to see him ever again. I hate
him. He makes me—" She thrust out her tongue; she really
felt overcome with nausea. The spot on her hand he had kissed that morning began to tingle again with unpleasant sensations. She said, "I'm not going back there. I shall stay with

104

you."

"Very fine. Very good," Maji said, and she laughed ironically.

She left her daughter's side and went back to sit by her harmonium. She began to play, but broke off after a few bars. She talked. Her voice rambled on. Sometimes she laughed, sometimes she sighed. Tara did not listen carefully, but it was good to hear the familiar voice and other familiar sounds as well—the incessant beating of little hammers on metal from the street of the silversmiths, women calling to each other in lazy morning voices, and their slippers slipslopping along the stone floors.

Maji was talking about the dead old man. "Sometimes I couldn't stand him any more. Several times I drove him away. 'Don't show your face here again,' I said. Then he rolled up his few things and left. But sooner or later he always came back again. One day he would be there, and I would say, 'Oh, you have come.' And then he stayed."

Tara yawned. The subject was not interesting to her; the old man had always been there, like this mattress, like that birdcage.

Maji said, "This is what happened one night. It was long ago, when I was still young and had visitors. We were sitting; I was singing. A few people were there. Your grandmother was there too. She sat and listened, with her head going up and down to my singing. Then a man came in—I think he had been upstairs with Phul Devi. Perhaps his business with her was finished, or perhaps they had thrown him out. He was a very third-class person, and his behaviour was also very third-class. Everyone told him to leave, but he said why should he leave—he was ready to spend money too. He drew a big bundle out of his pocket, but he only threw down one or

105

two rupees. 'Here,' he said. 'Take it, be quick.' And Grandmother was quick; she picked up the money at once and tucked it away. I was ready to continue singing, but he would not
let me. He touched me in a coarse way. I said, 'Please leave.' I
hoped the old man would do something—I say old man, but
of course he was young then—but all he did was play his
drum a bit louder, with his head down, and pretended to be
too busy to hear or see anything. I felt angry with him,
because it was his duty to make this person leave. Why else
did we keep him and give him all that food and let him live
here in the room with us? But he did nothing, he was afraid,
and I don't know what would have happened if Mithu had
not been here."

"Who?" Tara said out of her deep drowsiness.

"No, I have not spoken to you much about Mithu. It is long
ago." But Maji was smiling as if it were not long ago at all.
"Oh, he was a rascal, a layabout, no good at all. But that day
he was a blessing to us, for once. When this person would not
leave, Mithu slapped his face and then he pushed him out of
the door and gave him a kick down the stairs. Of course,
Mithu always loved a fight. But that day even your grandmother was quite pleased with him. And as for me—what
shall I tell you!" Maji flung her hands before her face.

Tara recognized her mother's feelings, and this sharpened
her own. "Is he always up there with Salima?" she asked.

"Leave it, Daughter," Maji counselled again.

"She must be giving him presents and money. He would
run anywhere, to anyone who can give him presents and
money, even if she were a hundred years old and ugly as the
devil."

"One thing I could not get out of my mind," Maji said.
"The way the old man had sat there playing the drum, with
106

his head bent down. I hated him for that. I could not put up with him one moment longer. So he had to roll up his little bundle again and go elsewhere. And then Mithu moved in. I did not care what your grandmother said. I would not listen to her, or to anyone. I was stone-deaf, except to *his* voice. And I thought this happiness would never come to an end."

Maji usually did not talk about things that were finished. Today, however, she went on and on, as if Tara did not have enough on her mind without having to hear all that.

"Then one day I found I was pregnant," Maji said. "God forgive me for everything I tried. But it was no use—you were determined to come and eat your share in this world. It was a very difficult time. There were complications; doctors and medicines had to be paid for. I lay here on this mat, and your grandmother wrung her hands and said we would all die. We cried day and night, not knowing where to turn. Don't ask about Mithu. With no clients, nothing going on, no food in the house, naturally it was too dull for him here. Then one day the old man was back again. Grandmother nearly fell over him on the stairs, where he was sleeping. She brought him in. You will say, What use was that, just one more belly to starve. Of course you are right, he couldn't help much. But he would get up very early—three, four o'clock, it must have been, though we never heard him, he went so quietly. He went to the wholesale fruit-and-vegetable market and bought bananas to sell from door to door. Why only bananas I don't know, but it brought in a little bit. We ate, and quite often there was even milk for me."

Tara sat up, her ears strained toward the stairs. She rushed to the door and opened it suddenly, as if trying to catch someone by surprise. But it was the wrong person.

"Who is it?" Maji said.

107

"Only that policeman who visits Roxana. I thought it was *him,* trying to sneak upstairs. Just let him try!" She clenched her teeth.

"Lie down. Rest yourself."

Tara lay down, but she did not rest. She said, "Everything will be different from now on. I shall be here, and then let me see how he goes upstairs."

She had spoken in a grim, threatening tone, but now this began to change. "Perhaps it is my fault also," she said in a forgiving voice. "He is a person you have to watch all the time. If the child goes astray, who is to be blamed? Not the child but the mother who has been failing in her duty." She did not look at Maji, whom she knew to be making a sceptical face. "When I am with him, he wants nothing and no one else. He is content. How often he has put his head here to rest and said, 'Now I am happy.' He loves my breasts very much. He says I carry two big pillows specially for him." She laughed and looked down at them, and then fidgeted them into position within her huge brassiere. "The elastic is going," she said. "I shall have to buy new brassieres. Leila also wrote to say send new ones. She sent a long list of things. Every day there is something new to buy and send."

"Well, thank God the money is there," Maji said, and invoked her usual blessings on Mukand Sahib. She ignored Tara's frowns. "He has been sent to us from above."

Tara laughed scornfully. "Yes, a fine angel," she said. Then, interpreting Maji's silence as a reproach, she cried, "You don't know! Day and night he is there, sitting there. And I have to sit with him so that he can look at me. He drops off to sleep, but if I try and move away he wakes up at once. 'Tara! Tara!' All the time I hear his voice calling, 'Tara! Tara!' Even in my dreams sometimes I think I hear him. And

108

when Leila is home from school, it is worst. I am with her for a few moments, and at once we hear 'Tara! Tara!' And Leila catches hold of me and says, 'Don't go.' But I have to go—to *run!*—because he is shouting so loud I'm afraid he will have a stroke." She clutched her head. "All I want is that he should leave me alone, leave me in peace," she pleaded. "I must have some *peace.*"

The door burst open. It was Bikki back again, triumphantly holding up some little earthenware pots. He wasted no time but set everything out for them to eat, talking all the while and telling them of acquaintances he had met in the bazaar and the conversation he had had with them. He began to eat with relish, commenting on the excellence of the pilao. He didn't notice that he was eating most of it. Tara was more interested in him than in the food. She kept stroking him, and he thought she was pleased with him because of what he had brought. This added to his own enjoyment, and he took more and more, saying, "Good, hmm?" and licked each of his fingers. Tara brought water for him to wash in, and she wiped his hands on a towel, and then she sat close to him again and ran her hands over his face and neck. She could not get enough of him. She toyed with his new gold chain and pulled it out of his shirt to look at. She held it in the palm of her hand, but she did not say anything, and tucked it back again and went on stroking him. At last she said to Maji, "No, I'm not going back."

Maji did not reply.

"Not going back where?" Bikki asked.

"Why should I?" Tara demanded of Maji, who still did not reply. "Maji is lonely," Tara said. "She wants me to come and live with her."

"Here?" Bikki asked, unable to keep a tremor out of his

109

voice.

"Yes." She was still fondling him, but now her caresses were those of a moody tigress. "Are you happy?" she asked him. "Now you will not have to come so far to visit me."

He nodded. Her caressing hand had got to his gold chain again. Again she drew it out and weighed it on her palm. "Who gave you this?" she asked him lightly.

After a moment, he said, "My auntie." He stared back at her boldly.

Maji began to speak in the ensuing silence. She talked about the old man. She said she had not expected him to die. He had always enjoyed excellent health, and right till the end he had kept up his good appetite. In fact, the day before he died he had asked for a sugar melon. But in these last months he could never bear to let her out of his sight. If she left him for five minutes, she would find him crying on her return. "With tears," she said, and with her fingers she showed how they had coursed their way down his cheeks. It had irritated her terribly.

But it was strange to be without him, she said. Sometimes she woke up in the night and called his name. Of course no one answered. She supposed she would get used to it in time—that is, if she still had time. No one was here forever. When your ticket of departure was issued to you, then you went. Well, she was packed and ready. Everything was in order. Her daughter was well settled—and as for the grand-daughter! There were just no words to describe the good fortune that girl was born with.

"You said you had to go and buy things to send to her school?" she asked Tara. "New brassieres? What else?"

Tara was still holding the end of Bikki's chain in her palm. Her hand was trembling. Bikki continued to look defiant. His

110

hard young eyes challenged her to say something further; but she dared not.

"What else?" Maji repeated stubbornly.

"Oh, so many things. Even a racket to play a game with."

"A princess!" Maji clapped her hands together in delight. She was full of gratitude for the favours showered on her family. First she cried out her thanks to God for them, and after that to Mukand Sahib.

Tara tucked Bikki's chain back into his shirt. He became good-humoured again and began to take an interest in the racket that had to be bought for Leila. Was it for tennis or badminton? He decided he had better go with Tara and help her buy it. He jumped up. "Let's hurry before the shops shut," he said. He always loved shopping.

Tara hesitated. She said Mukand Sahib would be waiting for her at home. He worried if she stayed away too long.

"Not long," Bikki said in a wheedling way. "We shall just go to the shops for the racket—and perhaps one or two other things for Leila."

Tara smiled. "Only for Leila?"

"Of course, if you see something you might like to give to me . . ." He shrugged, leaving the whole thing to her.

Tara looked at Maji as if for advice. Maji nodded. "Go along," she said. "Buy him something nice, and then you can go home."

Bikki bent down and kissed the bald patch on top of Maji's head. Almost before Maji could cry "Get out!", he was out of the door, pulling Tara along with him. Maji could hear them laughing together on the stairs, but she forgot them the next moment. She began to play the harmonium again and to sing a devotional song.

111

# TWO MORE UNDER THE
# INDIAN SUN

Elizabeth had gone to spend the afternoon with Margaret. They were both English, but Margaret was a much older woman and they were also very different in character. But they were both in love with India, and it was this fact that drew them together. They sat on the verandah, and Margaret wrote letters and Elizabeth addressed the envelopes. Margaret always had letters to write; she led a busy life and was involved with several organizations of a charitable or spiritual nature. Her interests were centred in such matters, and Elizabeth was glad to be allowed to help her.

There were usually guests staying in Margaret's house. Sometimes they were complete strangers to her when they first arrived, but they tended to stay weeks, even months, at a time—holy men from the Himalayas, village welfare workers, organizers of conferences on spiritual welfare. She had one constant visitor throughout the winter, an elderly government officer who, on his retirement from service, had taken to a spiritual life and gone to live in the mountains at Almora. He did not, however, very much care for the winter cold up there, so at that season he came down to Delhi to stay with Margaret, who was always pleased to have him. He had a soothing effect on her—indeed, on anyone with whom he came into contact, for he had cast anger and all other bitter passions out of his heart and was consequently always smiling and serene. Everyone affectionately called him Babaji.

He sat now with the two ladies on the veranda, gently rocking himself to and fro in a rocking chair, enjoying the winter sunshine and the flowers in the garden and everything about him. His companions, however, were less serene. Margaret, in fact, was beginning to get angry with Elizabeth. This happened quite frequently, for Margaret tended to be quickly irritated, and especially with a meek and conciliatory person like Elizabeth.

"It's very selfish of you," Margaret said now.

Elizabeth flinched. Like many very unselfish people, she was always accusing herself of undue selfishness, so that whenever this accusation was made by someone else it touched her closely. But because it was not in her power to do what Margaret wanted, she compressed her lips and kept silent. She was pale with this effort at obstinacy.

"It's your duty to go," Margaret said. "I don't have much time for people who shirk their duty."

"I'm sorry, Margaret," Elizabeth said, utterly miserable, utterly ashamed. The worst of it, almost, was that she really wanted to go; there was nothing she would have enjoyed more. What she was required to do was take a party of little Tibetan orphans on a holiday treat to Agra and show them the Taj Mahal. Elizabeth loved children, she loved little trips and treats, and she loved the Taj Mahal. But she couldn't go, nor could she say why.

Of course Margaret very easily guessed why, and it irritated her more than ever. To challenge her friend, she said bluntly, "Your Raju can do without you for those few days. Good heavens, you're not a honeymoon couple, are you? You've been married long enough. Five years."

"Four," Elizabeth said in a humble voice.

"Four, then. I can hardly be expected to keep count of each wonderful day. Do you want me to speak to him?"

"Oh no."

"I will you know. It's nothing to me. I won't mince my words." She gave a short, harsh laugh, challenging anyone to stop her from speaking out when occasion demanded. Indeed, at the thought of anyone doing so, her face grew red under her crop of grey hair, and a pulse throbbed in visible anger in her tough, tanned neck.

Elizabeth glanced imploringly towards Babaji. But he was rocking and smiling and looking with tender love at two birds pecking at something on the lawn.

"There are times when I can't help feeling you're afraid of him," Margaret said. She ignored Elizabeth's little disclaiming cry of horror. "There's no trust between you, no understanding. And married life is nothing if it's not based on the twin rocks of trust and understanding."

Babaji liked this phrase so much that he repeated it to himself several times, his lips moving soundlessly and his head nodding with approval.

"In everything I did," Margaret said, "Arthur was with me. He had complete faith in me. And in those days—Well." She chuckled. "A wife like me wasn't altogether a joke."

Her late husband had been a high-up British official, and in those British days he and Margaret had been expected to conform to some very strict social rules. But the idea of Margaret conforming to any rules, let alone those! Her friends nowadays often had a good laugh at it with her, and she had many stories to tell of how she had shocked and defied her fellow-countrymen.

"It was people like you," Babaji said, "who first extended the hand of friendship to us."

"It wasn't a question of friendship, Babaji. It was a question of love."

"Ah!" he exclaimed.

"As soon as I came here—and I was only a chit of a girl, Arthur and I had been married just two months—yes, as soon as I set foot on Indian soil, I knew this was the place I belonged. It's funny isn't it? I don't suppose there's any rational explanation for it. But then, when was India ever the place for rational explanations?"

Babaji said with gentle certainty, "In your last birth, you were one of us. You were an Indian."

"Yes, lots of people have told me that. Mind you, in the beginning it was quite a job to make them see it. Naturally, they were suspicious—can you blame them? It wasn't like today. I envy you girls married to Indians. You have a very easy time of it."

Elizabeth thought of the first time she had been taken to stay with Raju's family. She had met and married Raju in England, where he had gone for a year on a Commonwealth scholarship, and then had returned with him to Delhi; so it was some time before she met his family, who lived about two hundred miles out of Delhi, on the outskirts of a small town called Ankhpur. They all lived together in an ugly brick house, which was divided into two parts—one for the men of the family, the other for the women. Elizabeth, of course, had stayed in the women's quarters. She couldn't speak any Hindi and they spoke very little English, but they had not had much trouble communicating with her. They managed to make it clear at once that they thought her too ugly and too old for Raju (who was indeed some five years her junior), but also that they did not hold this against her and were ready to accept her, with all her shortcomings, as the will of God. They got a lot of amusement out of her, and she enjoyed being with them. They dressed and undressed her in new saris,

115

and she smiled good-naturedly while they stood round her clapping their hands in wonder and doubling up with laughter. Various fertility ceremonies had been performed over her, and before she left she had been given her share of the family jewelry.

"Elizabeth," Margaret said, "if you're going to be so slow, I'd rather do them myself."

"Just these two left," Elizabeth said, bending more eagerly over the envelopes she was addressing.

"For all your marriage," Margaret said, "sometimes I wonder how much you do understand about this country. You live such a closed-in life."

"I'll just take these inside," Elizabeth said, picking up the envelopes and letters. She wanted to get away, not because she minded being told about her own wrong way of life but because she was afraid Margaret might start talking about Raju again.

It was cold inside, away from the sun. Margaret's house was old and massive, with thick stone walls, skylights instead of windows, and immensely high ceilings. It was designed to keep out the heat in summer, but it also sealed in the cold in winter and became like some cavernous underground fortress frozen through with the cold of earth and stone. A stale smell of rice, curry, and mango chutney was chilled into the air.

Elizabeth put the letters on Margaret's work-table, which was in the drawing-room. Besides the drawing-room, there was a dining-room, but every other room was a bedroom, each with its dressing-room and bathroom attached. Sometimes Margaret had to put as many as three or four visitors into each bedroom, and on one occasion—this was when she had helped to organize a conference on Meditation as the Modern Curative—the drawing and dining-rooms too had been converted into dormitories, with string cots and bedrolls laid out end to end. Margaret was not only an energetic and active person involved in many causes but she was also the soul of generosity, ever ready to throw open her house to any friend or acquaintance in need of shelter. She had thrown it open to Elizabeth and Raju three years ago, when they had had to vacate their rooms almost over-night because the landlord said he needed the accommodation for his relatives. Margaret had given them a whole suite—a bedroom and dressing-room and bathroom—to themselves and they had had all their meals with her in the big dining-room, where the table was always ready laid with white crockery plates, face down so as not to catch the dust, and a thick white tablecloth that got rather stained towards the end of the week. At first, Raju had been very grateful and had praised their hostess to the skies for her kind and generous character. But as the weeks wore on, and every day, day after day, two or three times a day, they sat with Margaret and whatever other guests she had round the table, eating alternately lentils and rice or string-beans with boiled potatoes and beetroot salad, with Margaret always in her chair at the head of the table talking inexhaustibly about her activities and ideas—about Indian spirituality and the Mutiny and village uplift and the industrial revolution— Raju, who had a lot of ideas of his own and rather liked to talk, began to get restive. "But Madam, Madam," he would frequently say, half rising in his chair in his impatience to interrupt her, only to have to sit down again, unsatisfied, and continue with his dinner, because Margaret was too busy with her own ideas to have time to take in his.

117

Once he could not restrain himself. Margaret was talking about—Elizabeth had even forgotten what it was—was it the first Indian National Congress? At any rate, she said something that stirred Raju to such disagreement that this time he did not restrict himself to the hesitant appeal of 'Madam' but said out loud for everyone to hear, 'Nonsense, she is only talking nonsense.' There was a moment's silence; then Margaret, sensible woman that she was, shut her eyes as a sign that she would not hear and would not see, and, repeating the sentence he had interrupted more firmly than before, continued her discourse on an even keel. It was the other two or three people sitting with them round the table—a Buddhist monk with a large shaved skull, a welfare worker, and a disciple of the Gandhian way of life wearing nothing but the homespun loincloth in which the Mahatma himself had always been so simply clad—it was they who had looked at Raju, and very, very gently one of them had clicked his tongue.

Raju had felt angry and humiliated, and afterwards, when they were alone in their bedroom, he had quarrelled about it with Elizabeth. In his excitement, he raised his voice higher than he would have if he had remembered that they were in someone else's house, and the noise of this must have disturbed Margaret, who suddenly stood in the doorway, looking at them. Unfortunately, it was just at the moment when Raju, in his anger and frustration, was pulling his wife's hair, and they both stood frozen in this attitude and stared back at Margaret. The next instant, of course, they had collected themselves, and Raju let go of Elizabeth's hair, and she pretended as best she could that all that was happening was that he was helping her comb it. But such a feeble subterfuge would not do before Margaret's penetrating eye, which she

118

kept fixed on Raju, in total silence, for two disconcerting minutes; then she said, 'We don't treat English girls that way,' and withdrew, leaving the door open behind her as a warning that they were under observation. Raju shut it with a vicious kick. If they had had anywhere else to go, he would have moved out that instant.

Raju never came to see Margaret now. He was a proud person, who would never forget anything he considered a slight to his honour. Elizabeth always came on her own, as she had done today, to visit her friend. She sighed now as she arranged the letters on Margaret's work-table; she was sad that this difference had arisen between her husband and her only friend, but she knew that there was nothing she could do about it. Raju was very obstinate. She shivered and rubbed the tops of her arms, goose-pimpled with the cold in that high, bleak room, and returned quickly to the verandah, which was flooded and warm with afternoon sun.

Babaji and Margaret were having a discussion on the relative merits of the three ways towards realization. They spoke of the way of knowledge, the way of action, and that of love. Margaret maintained that it was a matter of temperament, and that while she could appreciate the beauty of the other two ways, for herself there was no path nor could there ever be but that of action. It was her nature.

"Of course it is," Babaji said. "And God bless you for it."

"Arthur used to tease me. He'd say, 'Margaret was born to right all the wrongs of the world in one go.' But I can't help it. It's not in me to sit still when I see things to be done."

"Babaji," said Elizabeth, laughing, "once I saw her—it was during the monsoon, and the river had flooded and the people on the bank were being evacuated. But it wasn't being

119

done quickly enough for Margaret! She waded into the water and came back with someone's tin trunk on her head. All the people shouted, 'Memsahib, Memsahib! What are you doing?' but she didn't take a bit of notice. She waded right back in again and came out with two rolls of bedding, one under each arm."

Elizabeth went pink with laughter, and with pleasure and pride, at recalling this incident. Margaret pretended to be angry and gave her a playful slap, but she could not help smiling, while Babaji clasped his hands in joy and opened his mouth wide in silent, ecstatic laughter.

Margaret shook her head with a last fond smile. "Yes, but I've got into the most dreadful scrapes with this nature of mine. If I'd been born with an ounce more patience, I'd have been a pleasanter person to deal with and life could have been a lot smoother all round. Don't you think so?"

She looked at Elizabeth, who said, "I love you just the way you are."

But a moment later, Elizabeth wished she had not said this. "Yes," Margaret took her up, "that's the trouble with you. You love everybody just the way they are." Of course she was referring to Raju. Elizabeth twisted her hands in her lap. These hands were large and bony and usually red, although she was otherwise a pale and rather frail person.

The more anyone twisted and squirmed, the less inclined was Margaret to let them off the hook. Not because this afforded her any pleasure but because she felt that facts of character must be faced just as resolutely as any other kinds of fact. "Don't think you're doing anyone a favour," she said, "by being so indulgent towards their faults. Quite on the contrary. And especially in marriage," she went on un-waveringly. "It's not mutual pampering that makes a

120

marriage but mutual trust."

"Trust and understanding," Babaji said.

Elizabeth knew that there was not much of these in her marriage. She wasn't even sure how much Raju earned in his job at the municipality (he was an engineer in the sanitation department), and there was one drawer in their bedroom whose contents she didn't know, for he always kept it locked and the key with him.

"I'll lend you a wonderful book," Margaret said. "It's called *Truth in the Mind*, and it's full of the most astounding insight. It's by this marvellous man who founded an ashram in Shropshire. Shafi!" She called suddenly for the servant, but of course he couldn't hear, because the servants' quarters were right at the back, and the old man now spent most of his time there, sitting on a bed and having his legs massaged by a granddaughter.

"I'll call him," Elizabeth said, and got up eagerly.

She went back into the stone-cold house and out again at the other end. Here were the kitchen and the crowded servants' quarters. Margaret could never bear to dismiss anyone, and even the servants who were no longer in her employ continued to enjoy her hospitality. Each servant had a great number of dependents, so this part of the house was a little colony of its own, with a throng of people outside the rows of peeling hutments, chatting or sleeping or quarrelling or squatting on the ground to cook their meals and wash their children. Margaret enjoyed coming out there, mostly to advise and scold—but Elizabeth felt shy, and she kept her eyes lowered.

"Shafi," she said, "Memsahib is calling you."

The old man mumbled furiously. He did not like to have his rest disturbed and he did not like Elizabeth. In fact, he

121

did not like any of the visitors. He was the oldest servant in the house—so old that he had been Arthur's bearer when Arthur was still a bachelor and serving in the districts, almost forty years ago.

Still grumbling, he followed Elizabeth back to the verandah. "Tea, Shafi!" Margaret called out cheerfully when she saw them coming.

"Not time for tea yet," he said.

She laughed. She loved it when her servants answered her back; she felt it showed a sense of ease and equality and family irritability, which was only another side of family devotion. "What a cross old man you are," she said. "And just look at you—how dirty."

He looked down at himself. He was indeed very dirty. He was unshaven and unwashed, and from beneath the rusty remains of what had once been a uniform coat there peeped out a ragged assortment of grey vests and torn pullovers into which he had bundled himself for the winter.

"It's hard to believe," Margaret said, "that this old scarecrow is a terrible, terrible snob. You know why he doesn't like you, Elizabeth? Because you're married to an Indian."

Elizabeth smiled and blushed. She admired Margaret's forthrightness.

"He thinks you've let down the side. He's got very firm principles. As a matter of fact, he thinks I've let down the side too. All his life he's longed to work for a real memsahib, the sort that entertains other memsahibs to tea. Never forgave Arthur for bringing home little Margaret."

The old man's face began working strangely. His mouth and stubbled cheeks twitched, and then sounds started coming that rose and fell—now distinct, now only a mutter and a

122

drone—like waves of the sea. He spoke partly in English and partly in Hindi, and it was some time before it could be made out that he was telling some story of the old days—a party at the Gymkhana Club for which he had been hired as an additional waiter. The sahib who had given the party, a Major Waterford, had paid him not only his wages but also a tip of two rupees. He elaborated on this for some time, dwelling on the virtues of Major Waterford and also of Mrs Waterford, a very fine lady who had made her servants wear white gloves when they served at table.

"Very grand," said Margaret with an easy laugh. "You run along now and get our tea."

"There was a little Missie sahib too. She had two ayahs, and every year they were given four saris and one shawl for the winter."

"Tea, Shafi," Margaret said more firmly, so that the old man, who knew every inflection in his mistress's voice, saw it was time to be off.

"Arthur and I've spoiled him outrageously," Margaret said. "We spoiled all our servants."

"God will reward you," said Babaji.

"We could never think of them as servants, really. They were more our friends. I've learned such a lot from Indian servants. They're usually rogues, but underneath all that they have beautiful characters. They're very religious, and they have a lot of philosophy—you'd be surprised. We've had some fascinating conversations. You ought to keep a servant, Elizabeth—I've told you so often." When she saw Elizabeth was about to answer something, she said, "And don't say you can't afford it. Your Raju earns enough, I'm sure, and they're very cheap."

"We don't need one," Elizabeth said apologetically. There

123

were just the two of them, and they lived in two small rooms. Sometimes Raju also took it into his head that they needed a servant, and once he had even gone to the extent of hiring an undernourished little boy from the hills. On the second day, however, the boy was discovered rifling the pockets of Raju's trousers while their owner was having his bath, so he was dismissed on the spot. To Elizabeth's relief, no attempt at replacing him was ever made.

"If you had one you could get around a bit more," Margaret said. "Instead of always having to dance attendance on your husband's mealtimes. I suppose that's why you don't want to take those poor little children to Agra?"

"It's not that I don't want to," Elizabeth said hopelessly.

"Quite apart from anything else, you ought to be longing to get around and see the country. What do you know, what will you ever know, if you stay in one place all the time?"

"One day you will come and visit me in Almora," Babaji said.

"Oh Babaji, I'd love to!" Elizabeth exclaimed.

"Beautiful," he said, spreading his hands to describe it all. "The mountains, trees, clouds . . ." Words failed him, and he could only spread his hands farther and smile into the distance, as if he saw a beautiful vision there.

Elizabeth smiled with him. She saw it too, although she had never been there: the mighty mountains, the grandeur and the peace, the abode of Shiva where he sat with the rivers flowing from his hair. She longed to go, and to so many other places she had heard and read about. But the only place away from Delhi where she had ever been was Ankhpur, to stay with Raju's family.

Margaret began to tell about all the places she had been to. She and Arthur had been posted from district to district, in

124

many different parts of the country, but even that hadn't been enough for her. She had to see everything. She had no fears about travelling on her own, and had spent weeks tramping around in the mountains, with a shawl thrown over her shoulders and a stick held firmly in her hand. She had travelled many miles by any mode of transport available—train, bus, cycle, rickshaw, or even bullock cart—in order to see some little-known and almost inaccessible temple or cave or tomb. Once she had sprained her ankle and lain all alone for a week in a derelict rest house, deserted except for one decrepit old watchman, who had shared his meals with her.

"That's the way to get to know a country," she declared. Her cheeks were flushed with the pleasure of remembering everything she had done.

Elizabeth agreed with her. Yet although she herself had done none of these things, she did not feel that she was on that account cut off from all knowledge. There was much to be learned from living with Raju's family in Ankhpur, much to be learned from Raju himself. Yes, he was her India! She felt like laughing when this thought came to her. But it was true.

"Your trouble is," Margaret suddenly said, "you let Raju bully you. He's got something of that in his character—don't contradict. I've studied him. If you were to stand up to him more firmly, you'd both be happier."

Again Elizabeth wanted to laugh. She thought of the nice times she and Raju often had together. He had invented a game of cricket that they could play in their bedroom between the steel almirah and the opposite wall. They played it with a rubber ball and a hairbrush, and three steps made a run. Raju's favourite trick was to hit the ball under the bed,

125

and while she lay flat on the floor groping for it he made run after run, exhorting her with mocking cries of "Hurry up! Where is it? Can't you find it?" His eyes glittered with the pleasure of winning; his shirt was off, and drops of perspiration trickled down his smooth, dark chest.

"You should want to do something for those poor children!" Margaret shouted.

"I do want to. You know I do."

"I don't know anything of the sort. All I see is you leading an utterly useless, selfish life. I'm disappointed in you, Elizabeth. When I first met you, I had such high hopes of you. I thought, Ah, here at last is a serious person. But you're not serious at all. You're as frivolous as any of those girls that come here and spend their days playing mahjong."

Elizabeth was ashamed. The worst of it was she really had once been a serious person. She had been a school teacher in England, and devoted to her work and her children, on whom she had spent far more time and care than was necessary in the line of duty. And, over and above that, she had put in several evenings a week visiting old people who had no one to look after them. But all that had come to an end once she met Raju.

"It's criminal to be in India and not be committed," Margaret went on. "There isn't much any single person can do, of course, but to do nothing at all—no, I wouldn't be able to sleep at nights."

And Elizabeth slept not only well but happily, blissfully! Sometimes she turned on the light just for the pleasure of looking at Raju lying beside her. He slept like a child, with the pillow bundled under his cheek and his mouth slightly open, as if he were smiling.

"But what are you laughing at!" Margaret shouted.

126

"I'm not, Margaret." She hastily composed her face. She hadn't been aware of it, but probably she had been smiling at the image of Raju asleep.

Margaret abruptly pushed back her chair. Her face was red and her hair dishevelled, as if she had been in a fight. Elizabeth half rose in her chair, aghast at whatever it was she had done and eager to undo it.

"Don't follow me," Margaret said. "If you do, I know I'm going to behave badly and I'll feel terrible afterwards. You can stay here or you can go home, but *don't follow me.*"

She went inside the house, and the screen door banged after her. Elizabeth sank down into her chair and looked helplessly at Babaji.

He had remained as serene as ever. Gently he rocked himself in his chair. The winter afternoon was drawing to its close, and the sun, caught between two trees, was beginning to contract into one concentrated area of gold. Though the light was failing, the garden remained bright and gay with all its marigolds, its phlox, its pansies, and its sweet peas. Babaji enjoyed it all. He sat wrapped in his woollen shawl, with his feet warm in thick knitted socks and sandals.

"She is a hot-tempered lady," he said, smiling and forgiving. "But good, good."

"Oh, I know," Elizabeth said. "She's an angel. I feel so bad that I should have upset her. Do you think I ought to go after her?"

"A heart of gold," said Babaji.

"I know it." Elizabeth bit her lip in vexation at herself.

Shafi came out with the tea tray. Elizabeth removed some books to clear the little table for him, and Babaji said, "Ah," in pleasurable anticipation. But Shafi did not put the tray

127

down.

"Where is she?" he said.

"It's all right, Shafi. She's just coming. Put it down, please."

The old man nodded and smiled in a cunning, superior way. He clutched his tray more tightly and turned back into the house. He had difficulty in walking, not only because he was old and infirm but also because the shoes he wore were too big for him and had no laces.

"Shafi!" Elizabeth called after him. "Babaji wants his tea!" But he did not even turn round. He walked straight up to Margaret's bedroom and kicked the door and shouted, "I've brought it!"

Elizabeth hurried after him. She felt nervous about going into Margaret's bedroom after having been so explicitly forbidden to follow her. But Margaret only looked up briefly from where she was sitting on her bed, reading a letter, and said, "Oh, it's you," and "Shut the door." When he had put down the tea, Shafi went out again and the two of them were left alone.

Margaret's bedroom was quite different from the rest of the house. The other rooms were all bare and cold, with a minimum of furniture standing around on the stone floors; there were a few isolated pictures hung up here and there on the whitewashed walls, but nothing more intimate than portraits of Mahatma Gandhi and Sri Ramakrishna and a photograph of the inmates of Mother Theresa's Home. But Margaret's room was crammed with a lot of comfortable, solid old furniture, dominated by the big double bed in the centre, which was covered with a white bedcover and a mosquito curtain on the top like a canopy. A log fire burned in the grate, and there were photographs everywhere—family

128

photos of Arthur and Margaret, of Margaret as a little girl, and of her parents and her sister and her school and her friends. The stale smell of food pervading the rest of the house stopped short of this room, which was scented very pleasantly by woodsmoke and lavender water. There was an umbrella stand that held several alpenstocks, a tennis racket, and a hockey stick.

"It's from my sister," Margaret said, indicating the letter she was reading. "She lives out in the country and they've been snowed under again. She's got a pub."

"How lovely."

"Yes, it's a lovely place. She's always wanted me to come and run it with her. But I couldn't live in England any more, I couldn't bear it."

"Yes, I know what you mean."

"What do you know? You've only been here a few years. Pour the tea, there's a dear."

"Babaji was wanting a cup."

"To hell with Babaji."

She took off her sandals and lay down on the bed, leaning against some fat pillows that she had propped against the headboard. Elizabeth had noticed before that Margaret was always more relaxed in her own room than anywhere else. Not all her visitors were allowed into this room—in fact, only a chosen few. Strangely enough, Raju had been one of these when he and Elizabeth had stayed in the house. But he had never properly appreciated the privilege; either he sat on the edge of a chair and made signs to Elizabeth to go or he wandered restlessly round the room, looking at all the photographs or taking out the tennis racket and executing imaginary services with it; till Margaret told him to sit down and not make them all nervous, and then he looked sulky and

129

made even more overt signs to Elizabeth.

"I brought my sister out here once," Margaret said. "But she couldn't stand it. Couldn't stand anything—the climate, the water, the food. Everything made her ill. There are people like that. Of course, I'm just the opposite. You like it here too, don't you?"

"Very, very much."

"Yes, I can see you're happy."

Margaret looked at her so keenly that Elizabeth tried to turn away her face slightly. She did not want anyone to see too much of her tremendous happiness. She felt somewhat ashamed of herself for having it—not only because she knew she didn't deserve it but also because she did not consider herself quite the right kind of person to have it. She had been over thirty when she met Raju and had not expected much more out of life than had up till then been given to her.

Margaret lit a cigarette. She never smoked except in her own room. She puffed slowly, luxuriously. Suddenly she said, "He doesn't like me, does he?"

"Who?"

"'Who?'" she repeated impatiently. "Your Raju, of course."

Elizabeth flushed with embarrassment. "How you talk, Margaret," she murmured deprecatingly, not knowing what else to say.

"I know he doesn't," Margaret said. "I can always tell."

She sounded so sad that Elizabeth wished she could lie to her and say that no, Raju loved her just as everyone else did. But she could not bring herself to it. She thought of the way he usually spoke of Margaret. He called her by rude names and made coarse jokes about her, at which he laughed like a schoolboy and tried to make Elizabeth laugh with him; and

130

the terrible thing was sometimes she did laugh, not because she wanted to or because what he said amused her but because it was he who urged her to, and she always found it difficult to refuse him anything. Now when she thought of this compliant laughter of hers she was filled with anguish, and she began unconsciously to wring her hands, the way she always did at such secretly appalling moments.

But Margaret was having thoughts of her own, and was smiling to herself. She said, "You know what was my happiest time of all in India? About ten years ago, when I went to stay in Swami Vishwananda's ashram."

Elizabeth was intensely relieved at the change of subject, though somewhat puzzled by its abruptness.

"We bathed in the river and we walked in the mountains. It was a time of such freedom, such joy. I've never felt like that before or since. I didn't have a care in the world and I felt so—light. I can't describe it—as if my feet didn't touch the ground."

"Yes, yes!" Elizabeth said eagerly, for she thought she recognized the feeling.

"In the evenings we all sat with Swamiji. We talked about everything under the sun. He laughed and joked with us, and sometimes he sang. I don't know what happened to me when he sang. The tears came pouring down my face, but I was so happy I thought my heart would melt away."

"Yes," Elizabeth said again.

"That's him over there." She nodded towards a small framed photograph on the dressing-table. Elizabeth picked it up. He did not look different from the rest of India's holy men—naked to the waist, with long hair and burning eyes.

"Not that you can tell much from a photo," Margaret said.

131

She held out her hand for it, and then she looked at it herself, with a very young expression on her face. "He was such fun to be with, always full of jokes and games. When I was with him, I used to feel—I don't know—like a flower or a bird." She laughed gaily, and Elizabeth with her.

"Does Raju make you feel like that?"

Elizabeth stopped laughing and looked down into her lap. She tried to make her face very serious so as not to give herself away.

"Indian men have such marvellous eyes," Margaret said. "When they look at you, you can't help feeling all young and nice. But of course your Raju thinks I'm just a fat, ugly old memsahib."

"Margaret, Margaret!"

Margaret stubbed out her cigarette and, propelling herself with a very young expression on her face. "He was such fun poor old Babaji waiting for his tea."

She poured it for him and went out with the cup. Elizabeth went after her. Babaji was just as they had left him, except that now the sun, melting away between the trees behind him, was even more intensely gold and provided a heavenly background, as if to a saint in a picture, as he sat there at peace in his rocking chair.

Margaret fussed over him. She stirred his tea and she arranged his shawl more securely over his shoulders. Then she said, "I've got an idea, Babaji." She hooked her foot round a stool and drew it close to his chair and sank down on it, one hand laid on his knee. "You and I'll take those children up to Agra. Would you like that? A little trip?" She looked up into his face and was eager and bright. "We'll have a grand time. We'll hire a bus, and we'll have singing and games all the way. You'll love it." She squeezed his knee in

132

anticipatory joy, and he smiled at her and his thin old hand came down on the top of her head in a gesture of affection or blessing.

# PICNIC WITH MOONLIGHT
## AND MANGOES

Unfortunately the town in which Sri Prakash lived was a small one so that everyone knew what had happened to him. At first he did not go out at all, on account of feeling so ashamed; but, as the weeks dragged on, sitting at home became very dreary. He also began to realize that, with thinking and solitude, he was probably exaggerating the effect of his misfortune on other people. Misfortune could befall anyone, any time; there was really no need to be ashamed. So one morning when his home seemed particularly depressing he made up his mind to pay a visit to the coffee house. He left while his wife was having her bath—he told her he was going, he shouted it through the bathroom door, and if she did not hear above the running water that was obviously not his fault.

So when he came home and she asked him where he had been, he could say "I *told* you" with a perfectly good conscience. He was glad of that because he could see she had been worried about him. While she served him his food, he did his best to reassure her. He told her how pleased they had all been to see him in the coffee house. Even the waiter had been pleased and had brought his usual order without having to be told. His wife said nothing but went on patiently serving him. Then he began somewhat to exaggerate the heartiness of the welcome he had received. He said things which, though not strictly true, had a good effect—not so much on her (she continued silently to serve him) as on himself. By the time he had finished eating and talking, he was perfectly

134

reassured as to what had happened that morning. The little cloud of unease with which he had come home was dispelled. He realized now that no one had looked at him queerly, and that there had been no undertones in their "Just see who is here." It was only his over-sensitive nature that had made it seem like that.

He had always had a very sensitive nature: a poet's temperament. He was proud of it, but there was no denying that it had been the cause of many troubles to him—including the present one. The facts of the case were these: Sri Prakash, a gazetted government officer, had been suspended from his post in the State Ministry of Telecommunication while an inquiry was instituted regarding certain accusations against him. These were based on the words of a man who was a drunkard, a liar, and a convicted perjurer. His name was Goel and he was the father of a Miss Nimmi. Miss Nimmi had come to Sri Prakash to enquire about a possible vacancy as typist in his office. Sri Prakash had sincerely tried to help the girl, calling her for interviews several times, and the result of his good intentions had been that she had complained of his misbehaviour towards her. The father, after visiting Sri Prakash both in his office and at home and finding him not the man to yield to blackmail and extortion, had carried the complaint to Sri Prakash's superiors in the department. From there on events had taken their course. Naturally it was all extremely unpleasant for Sri Prakash—a family man, a husband and father of three respectably married daughters—but, as he was always telling his wife, he had no doubts that in the end truth and justice would prevail.

She never made any comment when he said that. She was by nature a silent woman: silent and virtuous. How virtuous!

135

She was the ideal of all a mother and wife should be. He thanked God that he had it in him to appreciate her character. He worshipped her. He often told her so, and told everyone else too—his daughters, people in the office, sometimes even complete strangers (for instance, once a man he had shared a rickshaw with). Also how he was ready to tear himself into a thousand pieces, or lie down in the middle of the main bazaar by the clock tower and let all who came trample on him with their feet if by such an action he could save her one moment's anxiety. In this present misfortune there was of course a lot of anxiety. There was not only the moral hardship but also the practical one of having his salary held in arrears while the inquiry took its course. Already they had spent whatever his wife had managed to lay by and had had to sell the one or two pieces of jewelry that still remained from her dowry. Now they were dependent for their household expenses on whatever their sons-in-law could contribute. It was a humiliating position for a proud man, but what was to be done? There was no alternative, he could not allow his wife to starve. But when his daughters came to the house and untied the money from the ends of their saris to give to their mother, he could not restrain his tears from flowing. His daughters were not as sympathetic toward him as his wife. They made no attempts to comfort him but looked at him in a way that made him feel worse. Then he would leave them and go to lie down on his bed. His daughters stayed for a while, but he did not come out again. He could hear them talking to their mother, and sometimes he heard sounds like the mother weeping. These sounds were unbearable to him, and he had to cover his head with the pillow so as not to hear them.

136

After that first visit to the coffee house, he continued to go every day. It was good to meet his friends again. He had always loved company. In the past, when he was still king in his own office, people had dropped in on him there all day long. At eleven o'clock they had all adjourned to the coffee house where they had drunk many cups of coffee and smoked many cigarettes and talked on many subjects. He had talked the most, and everyone had listened to and applauded him. But nowadays everything was changed. It was not only that he could not afford to drink coffee or pay for his own cigarettes: other things too were not as they had been. He himself was not as he had been. He had always been so gay and made jokes at which everyone laughed. Once he had jumped up on the table and had executed a dance there. He had stamped his feet and made ankle-bell noises with his tongue. And how they had laughed, standing around him in a circle—his friends and other customers, even the waiters: they had clapped their hands and spurred him on till he had jumped from the table—hands extended like a diver—and landed amid cheers and laughter in the arms held out to catch him.

Although nothing like that happened now, he continued to visit the coffee house regularly every morning; soon he was going regularly every evening too. There was usually a large party of friends, but one evening when he went there was no one—only a waiter flicking around with his dirty cloth, and a silent old widower, a regular customer, eating vegetable cutlets. The waiter was surly—he always had been, even in the days when Sri Prakash had still been able to hand out tips—and it was only after repeated inquiries that he condescended to say that, didn't Sri Prakash know? Hadn't they told him? They had all gone to Moti Bagh for a moonlight

137

picnic with mangoes. Sri Prakash slapped his forehead, pretending he had known about it but had forgotten. It was an unconvincing performance and the waiter sneered, but Sri Prakash could not worry about that now. He had to concentrate on getting himself out of the coffee house without showing how he was feeling.

He walked in the street by himself. It was evening, there was a lot of traffic and the shops were full. Hawkers with trays bumped in and out of the crowds on the sidewalks. On one side the sky was melting in a rush of orange while on the other the evening star sparkled, alone and aloof, like a jewel made of ice. Exquisite hour—hour of high thoughts and romantic feelings! It had always been so for Sri Prakash and was so still. Only where was he to go, who was there to share with him the longing for beauty that flooded his heart?

"Oh-ho, oh-ho! Just see who is here!"

Someone had bumped against him in the crowd, now stood and held his arms in a gesture of affectionate greeting. It was the last person Sri Prakash would have wished to meet: Goel, the father of Miss Nimmi, his accuser, his enemy, the cause of his ruin and tears. Goel seemed genuinely delighted by this meeting; he continued to hold Sri Prakash by the arms and even squeezed them to show his pleasure. Sri Prakash jerked himself free and hurried away. The other followed him; he protested at this unfriendliness, demanded to know its cause. He claimed a misunderstanding. He followed Sri Prakash so close that he trod on his heels. Then Sri Prakash stood still and turned round.

"Forgive me," said Goel. He meant for treading on his heels; he even made the traditional self-humbling gesture of one seeking forgiveness. They stood facing each other. They were about the same height—both were short and plump,

138

though Goel was flabbier. Like Sri Prakash, he also was bald as a ball.

Sri Prakash could hardly believe his ears: Goel was asking him to come home with him. He insisted, he said he had some bottles of country liquor at home, and what good luck that he should have run into Sri Prakash just at this moment when he had been wondering what good friend he could invite to come and share them with him? When Sri Prakash indignantly refused, tried to walk on, Goel held on to him. "Why not?" he insisted. "Where else will you go?"

Then Sri Prakash remembered where everyone else had gone. The moonlight picnic at Moti Bagh was an annual outing. The procedure was always the same: the friends hired a bus and, together with their baskets of mangoes and crates of local whisky, had themselves driven out to Moti Bagh. They sang boisterous songs all the way. At Moti Bagh they cut up some of the mangoes and sucked the juice out of others. Their mouths became sticky and sweet and this taste might have become unpleasant if they had not kept washing it out with the whisky. They became very rowdy. They waited for the moon to rise. When it did, their mood changed. Moti Bagh was a famous beauty spot, an abandoned and half ruined palace built by a seventeeth-century prince at the height of his own glory and that of his dynasty. When the moon shone on it, it became spectral, a marble ghost that evoked thoughts of the passing of all earthly things. Poems were recited, sad songs sung; a few tears flowed. Someone played the flute—as a matter of fact, this was Sri Prakash who had always taken a prominent part in these outings. But this year they had gone without him.

Goel did not live in a very nice part of town. The bazaar,

139

though once quite prosperous, now catered mainly for poorer people; the rooms on top of the shops had been converted into one-night hotels. Goel's house, which was in a network of alleys leading off from this bazaar, would have been difficult to find for anyone unfamiliar with the geography of the locality. The geography of his house was also quite intricate, as every available bit of space—in the courtyard, galleries, and on staircase landings—had been partitioned between different tenants. Goel and his daughter Miss Nimmi had one long narrow room to themselves; they had strung a piece of string half-way across to serve as both clothes-line and partition. At first Sri Prakash thought the room was empty, but after they had been there for some time Goel shouted "Oy!" When he received no answer, he pushed aside the pieces of clothing hanging from the string and revealed Miss Nimmi lying fast asleep on a mat on the floor.

Goel had to shout several times before she woke up. Then she rose from the mat—very slowly, as if struggling up from the depths of a sea of sleep—and sat there, blinking. Her sari had slipped from her breasts, but she did not notice. She also did not notice that they had a visitor. She was always slow in everything, slow and heavy. Her father had to shout "Don't you see who has come!" She blinked a few more times, and then very, very slowly she smiled and very, very slowly she lifted the sari to cover her breasts.

Goel told her to find two glasses. She got up and rummaged around the room. After a time she said there was only one. Sri Prakash said it didn't matter, he had to go anyway; he said he was in a hurry, he had to catch a bus for Moti Bagh where his friends awaited him. He got up but his host pressed him down again, asking what was the point of going now, why not stay here, they would have a good time together.

140

"Look," Goel said, "I've got money." He emptied out his pockets and he did have money—a wad of bank notes, God knew where they had come from. He let Sri Prakash look his fill at them before putting them back. He said let's go to Badshahbad, we'll take the liquor and mangoes and we'll have a moonlight picnic of our own. He got very excited by this idea. Sri Prakash said neither yes nor no. Goel told Miss Nimmi to change into something nice, and she disappeared behind the clothes-line and got busy there. Sri Prakash did not look in that direction, but the room was saturated by her the way a store room in which ripe apples are kept becomes saturated by their savour and smell.

Badshahbad was not as far off as Moti Bagh—in fact, it was just at the outskirts of town and could be reached very quickly. It too was a deserted pleasure palace but had been built two centuries later than the one at Moti Bagh and as a rather gaudy imitation of it. However, now in the dark it looked just the same. The surrounding silence and emptiness, the smell of dust, the occasional jackal cry were also the same. At first Sri Prakash felt rather depressed, but his mood changed after he had drunk some of Goel's liquor. Goel was determined to have a good time, and Miss Nimmi, though silent, also seemed to be enjoying herself. She was cutting up the mangoes and eating rather a lot of them. The three of them sat in the dark, waiting for the moon to rise.

Goel fell into a reminiscent mood. He began to recall all the wonderful things he had done in his life: how he had sold a second-hand imported car for Rs.50,000, and once he had arranged false passports for a whole party of Sikh carpenters. All these activities had brought in fat commissions for himself—amply deserved, because everything had been achieved only through his good contacts. That was his

141

greatest asset in life—his contacts, all the important people he had access to. He ticked them off on his fingers: the Under Secretary to the Welfare Ministry, the Deputy Minister of Mines and Fuel, all the top officers in the income tax department . . . He challenged Sri Prakash, he said: "Name any big name, go as high as you like, and see if I don't know him."

Sri Prakash got excited, he cried: "My goodness! Big names—big people—whenever there was anything to be done, everyone said 'Ask Sri Prakash, he knows everyone, he has them all in his pocket.' Once there was a function to felicitate our departmental Secretary on his promotion. The principal organizers came to me and said 'Sri Prakash, we need a VIP to grace the occasion.' I replied, 'I will get you the Chief Minister himself, just wait and see.' And I did. I went to him, I said 'Sir, kindly give us the honour of your presence' and he replied 'Certainly, Sri Prakash, with pleasure.' There and then he told his secretary to make a note of the appointment."

"When I go into the Secretariat building," Goel said, "the peons stand up and salute. I don't bother with appointments. The personal assistant opens the big shot's door and says 'Sir, Goel has come.' They know I don't come with empty hands. I slip it under their papers, no word spoken, they don't notice, I don't notice. The figures are all fixed, no need to haggle: 1000 to an Under Secretary, 2000 to a Deputy. Each has his price."

Goel smiled and drank. Sri Prakash also drank. The liquor, illicitly distilled, had a foul and acrid taste. Sri Prakash remembered reading in the papers quite recently how a whole colony of labourers had been wiped out through drinking illicit country liquor. Nothing could be done for them, it had rotted them through and through.

Goel said: "Let alone the Secretaries, there are also the Ministers to be taken care of. Some of them are very costly. Naturally, their term is short, no one can tell what will happen at the next elections. So their mouths are always wide open. You must be knowing Dev Kishan—"

"Dev Kishan!" Sri Prakash cried. "He and I are like that! Like that!" He held up two fingers, pressed close together.

"There was some work in his Ministry, it was rather a tricky job and I was called in. I went to his house and came straight to the point. 'Dev Kishan Sahib,' I said—"

Sri Prakash suddenly lost his temper: "Dev Kishan is not this type at all!" When Goel sniggered, he became more excited: "A person like you would not understand a person like him at all. And I don't believe you went to his house—"

"Come with me right now!" Goel shouted. "We will go together to his house and then you will see how he receives me—"

"Not Dev Kishan!" Sri Prakash shouted back. "Someone else—not he—"

"He! The same!"

Although they were both shouting at the tops of their voices, Miss Nimmi went on placidly sucking mangoes. Probably the subject was of no interest to her; probably also she was used to people getting excited while drinking.

"As a matter of fact," Goel sneered, "shall I let you into a secret—his mouth is open wider than anyone's, they call him The Pit because he can never get enough, your Dev Kishan."

"I don't believe you," Sri Prakash said again, though not so fervently now. He really had no particular interest in defending this man. It was only that the mention of his name had called up a rather painful memory.

143

When his troubles had first begun, Sri Prakash had run around from one influential person to another. Most people would not receive him, and he had had to content himself with sitting waiting in their outer offices and putting his case to such of their clerical staff as would listen. Dev Kishan, however was one of the few people who *had* received him. Sri Prakash had been ushered into his ministerial office which had two air conditioners and an inscribed portrait of the President of India. Dev Kishan had sat behind an enormous desk, but he had not asked Sri Prakash to take the chair opposite. He had not looked at Sri Prakash either but had fixed his gaze above his head. Sri Prakash wanted to plead, to explain—he had come ready to do so—if necessary go down on his knees, but instead he sat quite still while Dev Kishan told him that a departmental inquiry must be allowed to proceed according to rule. Then Sri Prakash had quietly departed, passing through the outer office with his head lowered and with nothing to say for himself whatsoever. He had not spoken for a long while afterwards. He kept thinking—he was still thinking—of the way Dev Kishan had looked above his head. His eyes had seemed to be gazing far beyond Sri Prakash, deep into state matters, and Sri Prakash had felt like a fly that had accidentally got in and deserved to be swatted.

Goel did not want to quarrel any more. He had come on a picnic, he had spent money on liquor and mangoes and the hiring of a horse carriage to bring them here. He expected a good time in return. He refilled their glasses while remembering other outings he had enjoyed in the past. He told Sri Prakash of the time he and some friends had consumed one dozen bottles of liquor at a sitting and had become very merry. He nudged Sri Prakash and said "Girls were also

144

brought." He said this in a low voice, so that Miss Nimmi would not hear, and brought his face close to Sri Prakash. Sri Prakash felt a desire to throw the contents of his glass into this face. He imagined that the liquor contained acid and what would happen. He was filled with such strong emotion that something, some release was necessary: but instead of throwing the liquor in his host's face, he emptied it on the ground in a childishly angry gesture. Goel gave a cry of astonishment, Miss Nimmi stopped half way in the sucking of a mango.

Just then the moon rose. The palace trembled into view and stood there, melting in moonlight. Sri Prakash left his companions and went toward it as one drawn toward a mirage. It did not disappear as he approached, but it did turn out to be locked. He peered through the glass doors and could just make out the sleeping form of a watchman curled up on the floor. The interior was lit only by the palest beams filtering in from outside. By day there were too many curlicued arches and coloured chandeliers, too many plaster leaves and scrolls: but now in the moonlight everything looked as it should. Overcome by its beauty and other sensations, Sri Prakash sat down on the steps and wept. He had his face buried in his hands and could not stop.

After a while Goel joined him. He sat beside him on the steps. Goel began to talk about the passing away of all earthly things, the death of kings and pariah dogs alike. He waved his hand toward the abandoned pleasure palace, he said "Where are they all, where have they gone?" Although these reflections were perfectly acceptable—probably at this very moment Sri Prakash's friends were making the same ones at their picnic in Moti Bagh—nevertheless, coming from Goel, Sri Prakash did not want to hear them. He felt

145

Goel had no right to them. What did he know of philosophy and history—indeed of anything except drinking and bribery? Sri Prakash lifted his head; irritation had dried his tears.

He said "Do you know what the Nawab Sahib Ghalib Hasan said when they came to tell him the enemy was at the gate?"

Goel did not know—he knew nothing—he hardly knew who the Nawab Sahib Ghalib Hasan was. To cover his ignorance, he waved his hand again and repeated "Where are they all, where have they gone?"

Sri Prakash began to instruct him. He knew a lot about the Nawab who had always been one of his heroes. Abandoning the palace at Moti Bagh, the Nawab had built himself this costly new palace here at Badshahbad and filled it with his favourites. There had been poets and musicians and dancing girls, cooks and wine tasters, a French barber, an Irish cavalry officer; also a menagerie which included a lion and an octopus. The Nawab himself wrote poetry which he read aloud to his courtiers and to the girls who massaged his feet and scented them. It was during such a session that messengers had come to tell him the enemy was at the gate. He had answered by reciting these verses which Sri Prakash now quoted to Goel: "*When in her arms, what is the drum of war? the sword of battle? nay, even the ancient whistle of bony-headed Death?*"

"Ah!" said Goel, laying his hand on his chest to show how deeply he was affected.

Quite pleased with this reaction, Sri Prakash repeated the quotation. Then he quoted more verses written by the Nawab. Goel turned out to be an appreciative listener. He swayed his head and sometimes shouted out loud in applause

146

the way connoisseurs shout when a musician plays a note, a dancer executes a step showing more than human skill. Sri Prakash began rather to enjoy himself. It had been a long time since anyone had cared to listen to him reciting poetry. His wife and daughters—he had always regretted it—had no taste for poetry at all; not for music either, which he loved so much.

But then Goel made a mistake. Overcome by appreciation, he repeated a line that Sri Prakash had just quoted to him: *"O rose of my love, where have your petals fallen?"* But Goel's voice, which was vulgar and drunken, degraded these beautiful words. Suddenly Sri Prakash turned on him. He called him all the insulting names he could think of such as liar, swindler, blackmailer, and drunkard. Goel continued to sit there placidly, even nodding once or twice as if he agreed. Perhaps he was too drunk to hear or care; or perhaps he had been called these names so often that he had learned to accept them. But this passive attitude was frustrating for Sri Prakash; he ran out of insults and fell silent.

After a while he said "Why did you do it? For myself I don't care—but what about my wife and family? Why should their lives be ruined? Tell me that."

Goel had no answer except a murmur of sympathy. As if grateful for this sympathy, Sri Prakash began to tell him moving incidents from his married life. They all illustrated the fact that his wife was an angel, a saint. The more Sri Prakash knew her the more he marvelled. In her he had studied all womanhood and had come to the conclusion that women are goddesses at whose feet men must fall down and worship. He himself had got into the habit of doing so quite often. Not now so much any more—his spirits were too low, he felt himself unworthy—but in the past when things were

147

still well with him. Then he would come home from a late night outing with friends to find her nodding in the kitchen, waiting for him to serve him his meal. He would be overcome with love and admiration for her. With a cry that startled her from her sleep, he would fall down at her feet and lift the hem of her garment to press it to his lips. Although she tried to make him rise, he would not do so; he wanted to stay down there to make it clear how humble he was in relation to her greatness. Then she undressed him right there where he lay on the floor and tried to get him to bed. Sometimes she had to lift him up in her arms—he had always been a small man—and he loved that, he lay in her arms with his eyes shut and felt himself a child enfolded in its mother's love. "Mother," he would murmur in ecstasy, as she staggered with him to the bed.

Goel had fallen asleep. Sri Prakash was sorry, for although he did not esteem Goel as a person, he felt the need of someone to talk to. Not only about his wife; there were many other subjects, many thoughts he longed to share. It was like that with him sometimes. His heart was so full, so weighted with feeling, that he longed to fling it somewhere—to someone—or, failing someone, up to the moon that was so still and looked down at him from heaven. But there *was* someone; there was Miss Nimmi. She had remained where they had left her by the basket of mangoes and the bottles. She had finished eating mangoes. She did not seem to mind being left alone nor did she seem impatient to go home but just content to wait till they were ready. She sat with her hands folded and looked in front of her at the bare and dusty earth.

This patient pose was characteristic of her. It was the way she had sat in Sri Prakash's office when she had come to ask him for a job. That was why he had kept telling her to come back: to have the pleasure of seeing her in his office, ready to wait for as long as he wanted. She had reminded him of a chicken sitting plump and cooked on a dish on a table. By the third day he had begun to call her his little chicken. "Fall to!" he would suddenly cry and make the motion of someone who grabbed from a dish and fell to eating. Of course she hadn't known what he meant, but she had smiled all the same.

"Fall to!" he cried now, as he joined her on the ground among the empty bottles. And now too she smiled. Like the palace floating behind her, she was transformed and made beautiful by moonlight. It veiled her rather coarse features and her skin pitted by an attack of smallpox in childhood.

He moved up close to her. Her breasts, as warm as they were plump, came swelling out of her bodice, and he put his hand on them: but respectfully, almost with awe, so that there was no harm in her leaving it there. "Where is Papa?" she asked.

"Asleep. You need not worry."

Very gently and delicately he stroked her breasts. Then he kissed her mouth, tasting the mango there. She let all this be done to her. It had been the same in his office—she had always kept quite still, only occasionally glancing over her shoulder to make sure no one was coming. She did the same now, glanced toward her father.

"You need not worry," Sri Prakash said again. "He has drunk a lot. He won't wake up."

"He *is* waking up."

They both looked toward Goel left alone in front of the palace. He was trying to stretch himself out more comfortably along the steps, but instead he rolled down them. It was

149

not far, and the ground seemed to receive him softly; he did not move but remained lying there.

"Is he all right?" Miss Nimmi asked.

"Of course he is all right. What could happen to *him*?" Sri Prakash spoke bitterly. He took his hand away from her; his mood was spoiled. He said "Why did you let him do it to me? What harm have I done to him? Or to you? Answer."

She had no answer. There was none, he knew. She could not say that he had harmed her, had done anything bad. Was it bad to love a person? To adore and worship the way he had done? Those moments in his office had been pure, and his feelings as sacred as if he were visiting a shrine to place flowers there at the feet of the goddess.

"Why?" he asked again. "What did I do to you?"

"That is what Papa kept asking: 'What did he do to you?' When I said you did nothing, he got very angry. He kept asking questions, he would not stop. Sometimes he woke me up at night to ask."

Sri Prakash pressed his face into her neck. "What sort of questions?" he murmured from out of there.

"He asked 'Where did he put his hand?' When I couldn't remember, he asked 'Here?' So I had to say yes. Because you did."

"Yes," he murmured. "Yes I did." And he did it again, and she let him.

She said "Papa shouted and screamed. He hit his head against the wall. But it wasn't only that—there were other things. He was going through a lot of other troubles at that time. Two men kept coming. They told him he would have to go to jail again. Papa is very frightened of going to jail. When he was there before, he came out *so* thin." She showed how with her finger. "He lost fifty pounds in there."

150

Sri Prakash remembered Goel's demented state in those days. He had come to him many times, threatening, demanding money; he had looked like a madman, and Sri Prakash—still sitting secure behind his desk then, safe in his office—had treated him like one. "Go to hell," he had told him. "Do what you like." And the last time he had said that, Goel had pounded the desk between them and thrust his face forward into Sri Prakash's: "Then you will see!" he had screamed. "You will see and learn!" He had really looked like a madman—even with foam at his mouth. Sri Prakash had felt uneasy but nevertheless had laughed in the other's face and blown a smoke ring.

Miss Nimmi said "I was very frightened. Papa was in a terrible mood. He said he would teach you a lesson you would not forget. He said 'Why should I be the only person in this world to suffer blows and kicks? Let someone else also have a few of these.' But afterwards those two men stopped coming, and then Papa was much better. He was cheerful again and brought me a present, a little mirror like a heart. And then he was sorry about you. He tried to go to your office again, to change his report, but they said it was too late. I cried when he came back and told me that."

"You cried? You cried for me?" Sri Prakash was moved.

"Yes, and Papa also was sad for you."

Goel was still lying at the foot of the steps where he had rolled down. Sri Prakash did not feel unkindly towards him—on the contrary, he even felt quite sorry for him. But his greatest wish with regard to him at the moment was that he would go on sleeping. Sri Prakash did not want to be disturbed in his private conversation with Miss Nimmi. In his mind he prayed for sufficient time, that they might not be interrupted by her father.

151

"I cried so much that Papa did everything he could to make me feel better. He brought me more presents—sweets and a piece of cloth. When still I went on crying, he said 'What is to be done? It is his fate.'"

"He is right," Sri Prakash said. He too spoke only to soothe her. He did not want Miss Nimmi to be upset in any way. He just wanted her to be as she always was and to keep still so that he could adore her to his heart's content. He raised the hem of her sari to his lips, the way he did to his wife; and he also murmured "Goddess" to her the way he did to his wife—worshipping all women in her, their goodness and beauty.

# IN A GREAT MAN'S HOUSE

The letter came in the morning, but when she told Khan Sahib about it, he said she couldn't go. There was no time for argument because someone had come to see him—a research scholar from abroad writing a thesis on Indian musical theory—so she was left to brood by herself. First she thought bad thoughts about Khan Sahib. Then she thought about the wedding. It was to take place in her home-town, in the old house where she had grown up and where her brother now lived with his family. She had a very clear vision of this house and the tree in its courtyard to which a swing was affixed. There was always a smell of tripe being cooked (her father had been very fond of it); a continuous sound of music, of tuning and singing and instrumental practice, came out of the many dark little rooms. Now these rooms would be packed with family members, flocking from all over the country to attend the wedding. They would all have a good time together. Only she was to be left here by herself in her silent, empty rooms—alone except for Khan Sahib and her thieving servants.

Later in the morning her sister Roxana, who of course had also had a letter, came to discuss plans. Roxana came with her eldest daughter and her youngest son and was very excited, looking forward to the journey and the wedding. She cried out when Hamida told her that Khan Sahib would not allow her to go.

Hamida said "It is the time of the big Music Conference.

153

He says he needs me here." She added: "For what I don't know."

Roxana shook her head at such behaviour. Then she inclined it towards Khan Sahib's practice room from which she could hear the sound of voices. She asked, "Who is with him?" Her neck was craned forward, her earrings trembled, she wore the strained expression she always did when she was poking into someone else's business, especially Khan Sahib's.

"An American," Hamida replied with a shrug. "He has come to speak about something scholarly with him. Don't, Baba," she admonished Roxana's little boy who was smearing his fingers against the locked glass cabinet in which she kept precious things for show.

Roxana strained to listen to the voices, but when she could not make out anything, she began to shake her head again. She said "He must allow. He can't say no to you."

"Very big people will be coming for the Conference."

"But a niece's wedding! A brother's daughter!"

"They will all be coming to the house to visit Khan Sahib. Of course someone will have to be there for the cooking and other arrangements. Who can trust servants," she concluded with a sigh.

Roxana, who had no servants, puckered her mouth.

"Don't, Baba!" Hamida said again to the child who was doing dreadful damage with his sticky fingers to her polished panes.

"He wants to play," Roxana said. "He will need some new little silk clothes for the wedding. And this child also," she added, indicating her meek daughter sitting beside her. The girl did look rather shabby, but Hamida gave no encouragement. So then Roxana nudged her daughter and said

154

"You must ask auntie nicely—nicely," and she leered to show her how. The girl was ashamed and lowered her eyes. Hamida was both ashamed and irritated. Her gold bangles jingled angrily as she unlocked her cabinet and took out the Japanese plastic doll Baba had been clamouring for. "Now sit quiet," she admonished him, and he did so.

Roxana leaned forward again with her greedy look of curiosity. Khan Sahib's visitor was leaving: they could hear Khan Sahib's loud hearty voice seeing him off from the front of the house. Then Khan Sahib returned into the house and walked through his practice room into the back room where the women sat. Roxana at once pulled her veil over her head and simpered. She always simpered in his presence: not only was he an elder brother-in-law but he was also the great man in the family.

Condescending and gracious, he did honour to both roles. He pinched the niece's cheek and swept Baba up into his arms. He laughed "Ha-ha!" at Baba who however was frightened of this uncle with the large moustache and loud voice. After laughing at him, Khan Sahib did not know what to do with him so he handed him over to Hamida who put him back on the floor.

"How is my brother?" he asked Roxana. He meant his brother-in-law—Roxana's husband—who was also a musician but in a very small way with a very small job in All India Radio.

"What shall I say: poor man," Roxana replied. It was her standard reply to Khan Sahib's queries on this subject. Her husband was a very humble, self-effacing man so it was up to her to be on the look-out on his behalf.

Hamida, who felt that all requests to Khan Sahib should come only through herself, did not wish to encourage this

155

conversation. In any case, she now had things of her own to say: "They are leaving next week," she informed her husband. "They are going by train. The others will also be leaving from Bombay at the same time. Everyone is going of course. Sayyida has even postponed her operation."

Khan Sahib said to Roxana "Ask my brother to come and see me. There may be something for him at the Music Conference."

"God knows it is needed. There will be all sorts of expenses for the wedding. For myself it doesn't matter but at least these children should have some decent clothes to go to my brother's house."

"Well well," Khan Sahib reassured her. He looked at the niece with a twinkle: he had very fat cheeks and when he was good-humoured, as now, his eyes quite disappeared in them. But when he was not, then these same eyes looked large and rolled around. He told Hamida: "You had better take her to the shops. Some pretty little pink veils and blouses," he promised the girl and winked at her playfully. "She will look like a little flower." He had always longed for a daughter, and when he spoke to young girls, he was tender and loving.

"I can leave her with you now," Roxana said with a sigh of sacrifice.

"No today I'm busy," Hamida said.

"See that you are a good girl," Roxana told the girl. "I don't want to hear any bad reports." She got up and adjusted her darned veil. "Come, Baba," she said. "Give that little doll back to auntie, it is hers."

Baba began to cry and Khan Sahib said "No no it belongs to Baba, take it, child." But Hamida had already taken it away from him and swiftly locked it back into her cabinet. She also lost no time in ushering her sister out of the house.

156

The girl followed them.

"When should I send him to you?" Roxana called back to Khan Sahib. He did not hear her because of Baba's loud cries; but Hamida said "I will send word."

"You can stay till tomorrow or even the day after if she needs you," Roxana told her daughter.

The girl had blushed furiously. She said "Auntie is busy."

Roxana ignored her and walked out with Baba in her arms. When the girl tried to follow, Hamida said "You can stay," though not very graciously. She didn't look at her again—she had no time, she had to hurry back to Khan Sahib. There was a lot left she had to say to him.

He was lying on his bed, resting. She said "I must go. What will people say? Everyone will think there has been some quarrel in the family."

"It is not possible." His eyes were shut and his stomach, rising like a dome above the bed, breathed up and down peacefully.

"But my own niece! My own brother's own daughter!"

"You are needed here."

She turned from him and began to tidy up his crowded dressing-table. Actually, it was very tidy already—she did it herself every morning—but she nervously moved a few phials and jars about while thinking out her next move. She could see him in the mirror. He looked like an immoveable mountain. What chance did she have against him? Her frail hands, loaded with rings, trembled. Then she began to tremble all over. She remembered similar scenes in the past—so many! so many!—when she had desperately wanted something and he had lain like that, mountainously, on his bed.

He said "Massage my legs."

She was holding one of his phials of scent. She was over-

157

come by the desire to fling it into the mirror—and then sweep all his scents and oils and hair-dyes off the table and throw them around and smash a lot of glass. Of course she didn't; she put the bottle down, though her hands trembled more than ever. Nowadays she always overcame these impulses. It had not been so in the past: then she had often been violent. Once she really had smashed all the bottles on his dressing-table. It had been a holocaust, and two servants had had to spend many hours cleaning and picking up the splinters. For weeks afterwards the room was saturated in flowery essences, and some of the stains had never come out. But what good had it done her? None. So nowadays she never threw things.

"The right leg," he said from the bed.

"I can't," she said.

"Tcha, you're useless."

She swung round from the mirror: "Then why do you want me here? If I'm useless why should I stay for your Conference!"

He continued to look peaceful. It was always that way: he was so confident, so relaxed in his superior strength. "Come here," he said. When she approached, he pointed at his right leg. She squatted by the side of his bed and began to massage him. But she really was no good at it. Even when she went to it with good will (which was not the case at present), her arms got tired very quickly. She also tended to become impatient quite soon.

"Harder, *harder*," he implored. "At least try."

Instead she left off. She remained on the floor and buried her head in his mattress. He didn't look at her but groped with his hands at her face; when he felt it wet, he clicked his tongue in exasperation. He said "What is the need for this?
158

What is so bad?"

Everything, it seemed to her, was bad. Not only the fact that he wouldn't let her go to the wedding, but so many other things as well: her whole life. She buried her head deeper. She said "My son, my little boy." That was the worst of all, the point it seemed to her at which the sorrow of her life came to a head.

It had been the occasion of their worst quarrel (the time when she had broken all his bottles). Khan Sahib had insisted that the boy be sent away for education to an English-type boarding school in the hills. Hamida had fought him every inch of the way. She could not, would not be parted from Sajid. He was her only child, she could never have another. His birth had been very difficult: she had been in labour for two days and finally there had to be a Caesarian operation and both of them had nearly died. For his first few years Sajid had been very delicate, and she could not bear to let him out of her sight for a moment. She petted him, oiled him, dressed him in little silk shirts; she would not let him walk without shoes and socks and would not let him play with other children for fear of infection. But he grew into a robust boy who wanted to run out and play robust games. When she tried to stop him, he defied her and they had tremendous quarrels and she frequently lost her temper and beat him mercilessly.

"He will be coming home for his holiday soon," Khan Sahib said. "He will be here for two weeks."

"Two weeks! What is two weeks! When my heart aches for him—my arms are empty—"

"Go now," said Khan Sahib who had heard all this before.

"You want only one thing: to take everything you can away from me. To leave me with nothing. That is your only

159

happiness and joy in life."

"Go go go," said Khan Sahib.

When she went into the other room, Hamida was surprised to see the girl sitting there. She had forgotten all about her. She was sitting very humbly on the edge of Hamida's grand overstuffed blue-and-silver brocade sofa. She was studying the photograph of Sajid, a beautiful colour-tinted studio portrait in a silver frame. When Hamida came in, she quickly replaced it on its little table as if she had done something wrong. And indeed Hamida picked it up again and inspected it for fingermarks and then wiped it carefully with the end of her veil.

"He is coming home soon for his holidays," she informed the girl.

"Then he will be there for the wedding?"

Hamida frowned. She said "It will be the time of the big Music Conference. His father will want him to be here." She spoke as if the wedding was very much inferior in importance and interest to the Music Conference.

"Look," she told the girl. She opened her work-basket and took out a fine lawn kurta which she was embroidering. "It is for him. Sajid." She spread it out with an air as if it were a great privilege for her niece to be allowed to look at it. And indeed the girl seemed to feel it to be so. She breathed "Oh!" in soft wonder. Hamida's work was truly exquisite; she was embroidering tiny bright flowers like stars intertwined with delicate leaves and branches.

"Can you do it?" Hamida questioned. "Is your mother teaching you?"

"She is not very good."

"No," Hamida said, smiling as she remembered Roxana's

160

rough untidy work. "She never worked hard enough. Always impatient to be off somewhere and play. Without hard work no good results are achieved," she lectured the girl.

"Please teach me, auntie," the girl begged, looking up at Hamida with her sad childish eyes. Hamida was quite pleased, but she spoke sternly: "You have to sit for many hours and if I don't like your work I shall unpick it and you will have to start again from the beginning. Well we shall see," she said as the girl looked willing and humble. Suddenly a thought struck her, and she leaned forward to regard her more closely: "Why are you so thin?" she demanded.

The girl's cheeks were wan—which was perhaps why her eyes looked so large. Her arms and wrists were as frail as the limbs of a bird. Hamida wondered whether she suffered from some hidden illness; next moment she wondered whether she got enough to eat. Oh that was a dreadful thought—that this child, her own sister's daughter, might not be getting sufficient food! Her father was poor, her mother was a bad manager and careless and thoughtless and not fit to run a household or look after children though she had so many.

Hamida began to question her niece closely. She asked how much milk was taken in the house every day; she asked about butter, biscuits, and fruit. The girl said oh yes, there was a lot of everything always, more than any of them could eat; but when she said it, she lowered her eyes away from her aunt like a person hiding something, and after a time she became quite silent and did not answer any more questions. What was she hiding? What was she covering up? Hamida became irritated with her and she spoke sharply now, but that only made the girl close up further.

The servant came in with a telegram. He gave it to Hamida who held it in one hand while the other flew to her beating heart. Wild thoughts—of Sajid, of accidents and hospitals—rushed around in her head. She went into the bedroom and woke up Khan Sahib. When she said telegram, he at once sat up with a start. His hands also trembled though he said that it was probably something to do with the Music Conference; he said that nowadays everything was done by telegram, modern people no longer wrote letters. She helped him put on his reading-glasses and then he slowly spelled out the telegram which continued to tremble in his hands.

But it was from Hamida's brother, asking her to start as soon as possible. Evidently they needed her help very urgently for the wedding preparations. Khan Sahib tossed the telegram into her lap and lay down to sleep again. Now he was cross to have been woken up. Hamida remained sitting on the edge of the bed. She was full of thoughts which she would have liked very much to share with him, but his huge back was turned to her forbiddingly.

She *had* to go. She could not not go. Her family needed her; she was always the most important person at these family occasions. They all ran around in a dither or sat and wrung their hands till she arrived and began to give orders. She was not the eldest in the family, but she was the one who had the most authority. Although quite tiny, she held herself very erect and her fine-cut features were usually severe. As Khan Sahib's wife, she was also the only one among them to hold an eminent position. The rest of them were as shabby and poor as Roxana and her husband. They were all musicians, but none of them was successful, and they eked out a living by playing at weddings and functions and taking in pupils and whatever else came their way.

"They really want me," she said to Khan Sahib's sleeping

back. Let him pretend not to hear, but her heart was so full—she had to speak. "Not like you," she said. "For you what am I except a servant to keep your house clean and cook for your guests." She gave him a chance to reply, but of course she knew he wouldn't. "Just try and get your paid servants to do one half of the work that I do. All they are good for is to eat up your rice and lick up your butter, oh at that they are first-class maestros if I were not there to see and know everything. Well you will find out when I have gone," she concluded.

To her surprise Khan Sahib stirred; he said "Gone where?"

Actually she had meant when I have gone from this earth, but now she took advantage of his mistake: "Gone to my brother's house for my niece's wedding, where else," she said promptly.

"You are not going."

"Who says no? Who is there that has the right to say no!" She shrieked on this last, but then remembered the girl in the next room. She lowered her voice—which however had the effect of making it more intense and passionate: "There is no work for me here. No place for me at all. Ever since you have snatched away my son from me, I have sat as a stranger in your house with no one to care whether I am alive or what has happened."

She was really moved by her own words but at the same time remained alert to sounds from the kitchen where the servant was up to God knew what mischief. There was no peace at all—not a moment for private thought or conversation—she had to be on the watch all the time. She got up from the bed and went into the kitchen. She looked at the servant suspiciously, then opened the refrigerator to see if he

163

had been watering the milk. When she saw the jug full of milk, she remembered the underfed girl in the next room. She gave some orders to the servant and became very busy. She made milk-shake and fritters. She enjoyed doing it—she always enjoyed being in her kitchen which was very well equipped with modern gadgets. She loved having these things and did not allow anyone else to touch them but looked after them herself as if they were children.

The girl said she wasn't hungry. She said this several times, but when Hamida had coaxed and scolded her enough, she began to eat. It was a pleasure to watch her, she enjoyed everything so much. Hamida suddenly did an unexpected thing—she leaned forward and tenderly brushed a few strands of hair from the girl's forehead. The girl was surprised (Hamida was not usually demonstrative) and looked up from her plate with a shy, questioning glance.

"You are like my Sajid," Hamida said as if some explanation were called for. "He also—how he loved my fritters—how he licks and enjoys. Oh poor boy, God alone knows what rubbish they give him to eat in that school. English food," she said. "Boiled—in water."

She stuck out her tongue in distaste. It was one of her disappointments that Sajid did not complain more about the school food. Of course when he came home he did full justice to her cooking, but when she tried to draw him out on the subject of his school diet, he did not say what she desired to hear. He just shrugged and said it was okay. He always called it "grub". "The grub's okay," he said. She hated that word the way she hated all the English slang words which he used so abundantly, deliberately, knowing she could not understand them (she had little English). "Grub," she mimicked—and translated into Urdu: "Dog's vomit." He

164

laughed. She would have liked to cry over his emaciated appearance, but the fact was he didn't look emaciated—his face was plump, and his cheeks full of colour.

Not like this poor girl. She looked at the child's thin neck, her narrow little shoulders; she sighed and said "You're seventeen now, you were born the year before father went." It was certainly time to arrange for her. Hamida thought wistfully how well she herself would be able to do so. She would make many contacts and look over many prospective families and choose the bridegroom very carefully. And then what a trousseau she would get together for her: what materials she would choose, what ornaments! There was nothing like that for a boy. Even now Sajid did her a big favour if he consented to wear one of the kurtas she embroidered for him. He preferred his school blazer and belt with Olympic buckle.

"I was married by seventeen," she told the girl. "So was Roxana, so were we all. Look at you—who will marry you—" She lifted the girl's forearm and held it up for show. The girl smiled, blushed, turned aside her face. Hamida began to question her again. "What does she give you in the morning? And then afterwards? And in between?" When the girl again became stubborn and silent, Hamida scolded her gently: "You can tell me. Don't I love you as much as she does, aren't you my own little daughter too, my precious jewel? Why hide anything from me?" She took the end of her veil and wiped a rim of milk from her niece's lips. She was deeply moved, so was the girl. They sat closer together, the niece leaned against her aunt shyly. "You must tell me everything," Hamida whispered.

"Last Friday—" the girl began.

"Yes?"

"They both cried." Her lip trembled but at Hamida's urging she went on bravely: "Baba had an upset stomach and she wanted to cook some special dish for him. But when she asked Papa for the money to buy a little more milk, he didn't have. So they both cried and we all cried too."

"And I!" Hamida cried with passion. "Perhaps I'm dead that my own family should sit and cry for a drop of milk!" Then she stopped short, frowning to recollect something; she said "She did come last Friday."

She remembered it clearly because she had got very cross with Roxana who had arrived in a motor-rickshaw for which Hamida had then had to pay. When Hamida had finished scolding, Roxana had asked her for a hundred rupees and then patiently listened to some more scolding. She cried a bit when Hamida finally said she could only have fifty, but when she left she was very cheerful again and knotted the fifty rupees into the end of her veil. Hamida had climbed on the roof to spy on her, and it was as she had suspected—when Roxana thought she was unobserved, she hailed another motor-rickshaw and went rattling off, with her veil fluttering in the wind. Hamida worried that the money might come untied; she almost had a vision of it happening and the notes flying away and Roxana not even noticing because she was enjoying her ride so much.

Khan Sahib was calling. He had woken up from his nap and required attendance. He informed Hamida that visitors were expected and that preparations would have to be made for their entertainment. When she asked when they were expected, he answered impatiently "Now, now." She made no comment or complaint. People were always coming to visit Khan Sahib. She took no interest in who they were but only

166

in what and how much they would eat. She sent in platters of food and refilled them when they came out empty. She rarely bothered to peep into the room and did not try to overhear any of their conversation. Besides food, her only other concern was the clothes in which Khan Sahib would receive them.

She scanned his wardrobe now, the rows and rows of kurtas and shawls. He needed a lot of fine clothes always—for his concerts, receptions, functions, meetings with Ministers and other important people. It was her responsibility to have them made and keep them in order and decide what he was to wear on each occasion. But if he was not pleased with her choice, he would fling the clothes she had taken out for him across the room. Then she would have to take out others, and it was not unlikely that they too would meet with the same fate. Sometimes the floor was strewn with rejected clothes. Hamida did not care much. She let him curse and shout and throw things to his heart's content; afterwards she would call the servant to come in and clear up, while she herself sat in the kitchen and drank a cup of tea to relax herself.

But today his mood was good. He put up his arms like a child to allow her to change his kurta, and stretched out his legs so she could pull off his old churidars and fit on the new ones. He was in such a jolly mood that he even gave her a playful pinch while she was dressing him; when she pushed him away, he cackled and did it again. She pretended to be angry but did not really mind. Actually she was relieved that such childish amusements were all he required of her nowadays. It had not always been so. When they were younger, they had rarely managed to get through his toilette without her having to submit to a great deal more than only pinching. But now Khan Sahib was too heavy and fat to be

167

able to indulge himself in this way.

She began to tell him about Roxana's family. She repeated what the girl had told her. "What is to become of them?" Hamida asked. She reproached him with not putting enough work in Roxana's husband's way. It was so easy for Khan Sahib—to arrange for him to accompany other musicians at concerts (Roxana's husband played the tabla) or help him to get students. Khan Sahib defended himself. He reminded her of the many occasions when he had arranged something for his brother-in-law who had then failed to turn up—either because he had forgotten or because he had become engrossed in some amusement.

Hamida had to admit "He is like that." She sighed, but Khan Sahib laughed: he was fond of his brother-in-law who in return adored, worshipped him. When Khan Sahib sang, his brother-in-law listened in ecstasy—really it was almost like a religious ecstasy, and tears of joy coursed down his face that God should allow human beings to reach so high.

"Brother too is the same," Hamida said. "How will they manage? The bridegroom's family will arrive and nothing will be done and we shall be disgraced. I *must* go."

Khan Sahib did not answer but stretched out one foot. She rubbed talcum powder into the heel to enable her to slip the leg of his tight churidars over it more easily.

"They are like children," she said. "Only enjoyment, enjoyment—of serious work they know nothing . . . Have you seen that poor child?" She jerked her head towards the room where the girl sat. "Seventeen years old, no word of any marriage, and thin as a dry thorn. Come here!" she called through the door. "In here! Your uncle wants to see you!"

The door opened very slowly. The girl slipped through and stood there, overcome. "Right in," Hamida ordered. The

168

girl pressed herself against the wall. Hamida, anxious for her to make a good impression, was irritated to see her standing there trembling and blushing and looking down at her own feet. "Look up," Hamida said sharply. "Show your face."

"Aie-aie-aie," Khan Sahib said. He spoke to the girl as if she were some sweet little pet; he also made sounds with his lips as if coaxing a shy pet with a lump of sugar. "You must eat. Meat. Buttermilk. Rice pudding. Then you will become big and strong like Uncle." He was the only one to enjoy the joke. "Bring me these," he said, pointing to something on his dressingtable.

When the girl didn't know what he meant, Hamida became more irritated with her and cried out impatiently "His rings! His rings!"

"Gently, gently," said Khan Sahib. "Don't frighten the child. That's right," he said as the girl took up the rings and brought them to him. He spread out his hands for her. "Can you put them on? Do you know which one goes where? I'll teach you. The diamond—that's right—on this finger, this big big fat finger—that's very clever, oh very good—and the ruby here on this one—and now the other hand . . ."

He made it a game, and the girl smiled a bit as she fitted the massive rings on to his massive fingers. Hamida watched with pleasure. She loved the way Khan Sahib spoke to the child. He never spoke like that to his wife. His manner with her was always brusque, but with this girl he was infinitely gentle—as if she were a flower he was afraid of breaking, or one of those soft, soft notes that only he knew how to sing.

Later, when his guests had arrived and everything had been prepared and sent into them where they reclined on carpets in the practice room, it was Hamida's turn to lie on

169

the bed. She felt very tired and had a headache. Such sudden fits of exhaustion came over her frequently. She was physically a very frail, delicate lady. She lay with the curtains drawn and her eyes shut; her temples throbbed, so did her heart. Sounds of music and conversation came from the front of the house but here, in these back rooms where she lived, it was quite silent. Often at such times she felt very lonely and longed to have someone with her to whom she could say "Oh I'm so tired" or "My head is aching." But she was always alone. Even when Sajid was home from school, he usually stayed with the men in the front part of the house, or went out to play cricket with his friends; and when he did stay with her, he clattered about and made so much noise—he was an active, vigorous boy—that her rest was disturbed and she soon lost her temper with him and drove him away.

But today, when she opened her eyes, she saw the girl sitting beside her on the bed. Hamida said "My head is aching" and the girl breathed "Ah poor auntie" and these words, spoken with such gentle pity, passed over Hamida like a cooling sea-breeze on a scorching day. In a weak voice she requested the girl to rub her temples with eau-de-cologne. The girl obeyed so eagerly and performed this task with so much tenderness and love that Hamida's fatigue became a luxury. The noise from the practice room seemed to come from far away. Here there was no sound except from the fan turning overhead. The silence—the smell of the eau-de-cologne—the touch of the girl's fingers soothing her temples: these gave Hamida a sense of intimacy, of being close to another human being, that was quite new to her.

She put up her hand and touched the girl's cheek. She said "You don't look like your mother." Roxana, though she was scrawny now, had been a hefty girl. Also her skin had been

170

rather coarse, whereas this girl's was smooth as a lotus petal. The girl's features too were much more delicate than Roxana's had ever been.

"Everyone says I look like—"

"Yes?"

"Oh no," the girl said blushing. "It's not true. You're much, much more beautiful."

Hamida was pleased, but she said depreciatingly "Nothing left now."

She sat up on the bed so that she could see herself in the mirror and the girl beside her. Their two faces were reflected in the heart-shaped glass surrounded by a frame carved with leaves and flowers; because it was dim in the room—the curtains were drawn—they looked like a faded portrait of long ago. It was true that there was a resemblance. If Hamida had had a daughter, she might have looked like this girl.

She fingered the girl's kameez. It was of coarse cotton and the pattern was also not very attractive. Hamida clicked her tongue: "Is this how you are going to attend the wedding?" But when she saw the girl shrinking into herself again, she went on "Your mother is to blame. All right, she has no money but she has no taste either. This is not the colour to buy for a young girl. You should wear only pale blue, pink, lilac. Wait, I'll show you."

She opened her wardrobe. The shelves were as packed and as neatly arranged as Khan Sahib's. She pulled out many silk and satin garments and threw them on the bed. The girl looked on in wonder. Hamida ordered her to take off her clothes and laughed when she was shy. But she respected her modesty, the fact that she turned her back and crossed her little arms over her breasts: Hamida herself had also been very modest always. It was a matter of pride to her that not

171

once in their married life had Khan Sahib seen her naked.

She made the girl try on many of her clothes. They all fitted perfectly—aunt and niece had the same childish body with surprisingly full breasts and hips. Hamida made her turn this way and that. She straightened a neckline here, a collar there, she turned up sleeves and plucked at hems, frowning to hide her enjoyment of all this activity. The girl however made no attempt to hide it—she looked in the mirror and laughed and how her eyes shone! But there was one thing missing still, and Hamida took out her keys and unlocked her safe. The girl cried out when the jewel boxes were opened and their contents revealed.

There were many heavy gold ornaments, but Hamida selected a light and dainty necklace and tiny star-shaped earrings to match. "Now look," she said, frowning more than ever and giving the girl a push towards the mirror. The girl looked; she gasped, she said "Oh auntie!" and then Hamida could frown no longer but she too laughed out loud and then she was kissing the girl, not once but many times, all over her face and on her neck.

At that moment Roxana came into the room. When she saw her daughter dressed up in her sister's clothes and jewels, she clapped her hands and exclaimed in joyful surprise. Hamida's good mood was gone in a flash, and the first thing she did was shut her jewel-boxes and lock them back into her safe. The girl became very quiet and shy again and sat down in a corner and began to take off the earrings and necklace.

"No leave it!" her mother told her. "It looks pretty." She held up another kameez from among those on the bed. "How about this one? The colour would suit her very well."

"Why did you come?" Hamida asked.

172

"There has been a telegram. We have to start at once. Brother says our presence is urgently required. This lace veil is very nice. Try it on. Why are you shy? It is your own auntie."

Hamida began to fold all the clothes back again. She felt terribly sad, there was a weight on her heart. She asked "When are you leaving?"

"Tomorrow morning. Husband has gone to the station to buy the tickets. It may be difficult to get seats for all of us together, but let's see."

"You're *all* going?"

"Of course." She told the girl "You can pack up your old clothes in some paper that auntie will give you."

"Khan Sahib has called brother-in-law to come for the Music Conference."

"It is not possible. He has to attend my niece's wedding. And you?" she asked. "When are you leaving?"

Hamida didn't answer but was busy putting her clothes back into her wardrobe.

"He says no?" Roxana asked incredulously. Then she cried out in horror: "Hai! Hai!"

"Naturally, it is not possible for me to go," Hamida said. "Do you know what sort of people will be coming for this Conference? Have you any idea? All the biggest musicians in the country and many from abroad also will be travelling all the way to be present."

Roxana deftly snatched another kameez from among the pile Hamida was putting away. The girl meanwhile had unhooked the earrings and necklace and silently handed them to her aunt. Hamida could see Roxana in the mirror making frantic faces and gestures at the girl; she could also see that the girl refused to look at her mother but turned her back on

173

her and began to take off Hamida's silk kameez.

Roxana said "Come quickly now—there is a lot to be done for the journey. You can keep that on," she said. "There is no time to change."

"Yes keep it on," Hamida said. The girl gave her aunt a swift look, then wore the kameez back again. She did not thank her but looked down at the ground.

Just as they were going, Hamida said "Leave her with me." She said it in a rush like a person who has flung all pride to the wind.

"She can come to you when we return," Roxana promised. "She can stay two-three days if you like . . . You want to stay with auntie, don't you? You love to be with her." She nudged the girl with her elbow, but the girl didn't say anything, didn't look up, and seemed in a hurry to leave.

When she was alone, Hamida lay down on the bed again. Khan Sahib seemed to be having a grand time with his visitors. She could hear them all shout and laugh. Whenever he spoke, everyone else fell silent to listen to him. When he told some anecdote, they all laughed as loud as they could to show their appreciation. He would be stretched out there like a king among them, one blue satin bolster behind his back, another under his elbow; his eyes would be twinkling, and from time to time he would give a twirl to his moustache. Of course he wouldn't have a moment's thought to spare for his wife alone by herself in the back room. He would also have completely forgotten about the wedding and her desire to go to it. What were her desires or other feelings to him?

She shut her eyes. She tried to recall the sensation of the girl's fingers soothing her headache, but she couldn't. The smell of the eau-de-cologne had also disappeared. All she could smell now was the thickly scented incense that came

174

wafting out of the practice room. She found she was still holding the jewelry the girl had returned to her. She clutched it tightly so that it cut into her hand; the physical pain this gave her seemed to relieve the pressure on her heart. She raised the jewelry to her eyes, and a few tears dropped on it. She felt so sad, so abandoned to herself, without anyone's love or care.

Khan Sahib was singing a romantic song. Usually of course he sang only in the loftiest classical style, but occasionally, when in a relaxed mood, he liked to please people with something in a lighter vein. Although it was not his speciality—others devoted their whole lives to this genre—there was no one who could do it better than he. He drove people mad with joy. He was doing it now—she could hear their cries, their laughter, and it made him sing even more delicately as if he were testing them as to how much ecstasy they could bear. He sang: "Today by mistake I smiled—but then I remembered, and now where is that smile? Into what empty depths has it disappeared?" He wasn't Khan Sahib, he was a love-sick woman and he suffered, suffered as only a woman can. How did he know all that—how could he look so deep into a woman's feelings—a man like him with many coarse appetites? It was a wonder to Hamida again and again. She was propped on her elbow now, listening to him, and she was smiling: yes, truly smiling with joy. What things he could make her feel, that fat selfish husband of hers. He sang: "I sink in the ocean of sorrow. Have pity! Have pity! I drown."

175

# DESECRATION

It is more than ten years since Sofia committed suicide in the hotel room in Mohabbatpur. At the time, it was a great local scandal, but now almost no one remembers the incident or the people involved in it. The Raja Sahib died shortly afterward—people said it was of grief and bitterness—and Bakhtawar Singh was transferred to another district. The present Superintendent of Police is a mild-mannered man who likes to spend his evenings at home playing card games with his teenage daughters.

The hotel in Mohabbatpur no longer exists. It was sold a few months after Sofia was found there, changed hands several times, and was recently pulled down to make room for a new cinema. This will back on to the old cinema, which is still there, still playing ancient Bombay talkies. The Raja Sahib's house also no longer exists. It was demolished because the land on which it stood has become very valuable, and has been declared an industrial area. Many factories and workshops have come up in recent years.

When the Raja Sahib had first gone to live there with Sofia, there had been nothing except his own house, with a view over the ruined fort and the barren plain beyond it. In the distance there was a little patch of villagers' fields and, huddled out of sight, the village itself. Inside their big house, the Raja Sahib and Sofia had led very isolated lives. This was by choice—his choice. It was as if he had carried her away to this spot with the express purpose of having her to himself, of feasting on his possession of her.

Although she was much younger than he was—more than thirty years younger—she seemed perfectly happy to live there alone with him. But in any case she was the sort of person who exudes happiness. No one knew where the Raja Sahib had met and married her. No one really knew anything about her, except that she was a Muslim (he, of course, was a Hindu) and that she had had a good convent education in Calcutta—or was it Delhi? She seemed to have no one in the world except the Raja Sahib. It was generally thought that she was partly Afghan, perhaps even with a dash of Russian. She certainly did not look entirely Indian; she had light eyes and broad cheekbones and a broad brow. She was graceful and strong, and at times she laughed a great deal, as if wanting to show off her youth and high spirits, not to mention her magnificent teeth.

Even then, however, during their good years, she suffered from nervous prostrations. At such times the Raja Sahib sat by her bedside in a darkened room. If necessary, he stayed awake all night and held her hand (she clutched his). Sometimes this went on for two or three weeks at a time, but his patience was inexhaustible. It often got very hot in the room; the house stood unprotected on that barren plain, and there was not enough electricity for air-conditioning—hardly even enough for the fan that sluggishly churned the hot air. Her attacks always seemed to occur during the very hot months, especially during the dust storms, when the landscape all around was blotted out by a pall of desert dust and the sky hung down low and yellow.

But when the air cleared, so did her spirits. The heat continued, but she kept all the shutters closed, and sprinkled water and rose essence on the marble floors and on the

177

scented grass mats hung around the verandas. When night fell, the house was opened to allow the cooler air to enter. She and the Raja Sahib would go up on the roof. They lit candles in coloured glass chimneys and read out the Raja Sahib's verse dramas. Around midnight the servants would bring up their dinner, which consisted of many elaborate dishes, and sometimes they would also have a bottle of French wine from the Raja Sahib's cellar. The dark earth below and the sky above were both silver from the reflection of the moon and the incredible numbers of stars shining up there. It was so silent that the two of them might as well have been alone in the world—which of course was just what the Raja Sahib wanted.

Sitting on the roof of his house, he was certainly monarch of all he surveyed, such as it was. His family had taken possession of this land during a time of great civil strife some hundred and fifty years before. It was only a few barren acres with some impoverished villages thrown in, but the family members had built themselves a little fort and had even assumed a royal title, though they weren't much more than glorified landowners. They lived like all the other land-owners, draining what taxes they could out of their tenant villagers. They always needed money for their own living, which became very sophisticated, especially when they began to spend more and more time in the big cities like Bombay, Calcutta, or even London. At the beginning of the century, when the fort became too rough and dilapidated to live in, the house was built. It was in a mixture of Mogul and Gothic styles, with many galleries and high rooms closed in by arched verandas. It had been built at great cost, but until the Raja Sahib moved in with Sofia it had usually remained empty except for the ancestral servants.

178

On those summer nights on the roof, it was always she who read out the Raja Sahib's plays. He sat and listened and watched her. She wore coloured silks and the family jewelry as an appropriate costume in which to declaim his blank verse (all his plays were in English blank verse). Sometimes she couldn't understand what she was declaiming, and sometimes it was so high-flown that she burst out laughing. He smiled with her and said, "Go on, go on." He sat cross-legged smoking his hookah, like any peasant; his clothes were those of a peasant too. Anyone coming up and seeing him would not have thought he was the owner of this house, the husband of Sofia—or indeed the author of all that romantic blank verse. But he was not what he looked or pretended to be. He was a man of considerable education, who had lived for years abroad, had loved the opera and theatre, and had had many cultivated friends. Later—whether through general disgust or a particular disappointment, no one knew—he had turned his back on it all. Now he liked to think of himself as just an ordinary peasant landlord.

The third character in this story, Bakhtawar Singh, really did come from a peasant background. He was an entirely self-made man. Thanks to his efficiency and valour, he had risen rapidly in the service and was now the district Superintendent of Police (known as the S.P.). He had been responsible for the capture of some notorious dacoits. One of these—the uncrowned king of the countryside for almost twenty years—he had himself trapped in a ravine and shot in the head with his revolver, and he had taken the body in his jeep to be displayed outside police headquarters. This deed and others like it had made his name a terror among dacoits and other proscribed criminals. His own men feared him no less, for he was known as a ruthless disciplinarian. But he

179

had a softer side to him. He was terribly fond of women and, wherever he was posted, would find himself a mistress very quickly—usually more than one. He had a wife and family, but they did not play much of a role in his life. All his interests lay elsewhere. His one other interest besides women was Indian classical music, for which he had a very subtle ear.

Once a year the Raja Sahib gave a dinner party for the local gentry. These were officials from the town—the District Magistrate, the Superintendent of Police, the Medical Officer, and the rest—for whom it was the greatest event of the social calendar. The Raja Sahib himself would have gladly dispensed with the occasion, but it was the only company Sofia ever had, apart from himself. For weeks beforehand, she got the servants ready—cajoling rather than commanding them, for she spoke sweetly to everyone always—and had all the china and silver taken out. When the great night came, she sparkled with excitement. The guests were provincial, dreary, unrefined people, but she seemed not to notice that. She made them feel that their presence was a tremendous honour for her. She ran around to serve them and rallied her servants to carry in a succession of dishes and wines. Inspired by her example, the Raja Sahib also rose to the occasion. He was an excellent raconteur and entertained his guests with witty anecdotes and Urdu couplets, and sometimes even with quotations from the English poets. They applauded him not because they always understood what he was saying but because he was the Raja Sahib. They were delighted with the entertainment, and with themselves for having risen high enough in the world to be invited. There were not many women present, for most of the wives were too uneducated to be brought out into society.

Those that came sat very still in their best georgette saris and cast furtive glances at their husbands.

After Bakhtawar Singh was posted to the district as the new S.P., he was invited to the Raja Sahib's dinner. He came alone, his wife being unfit for society, and as soon as he entered the house it was obvious that he was a man of superior personality. He had a fine figure, intelligent eyes, and a bristling moustache. He moved with pride, even with some pomp—certainly a man who knew his own value. He was not put out in the least by the grand surroundings but enjoyed everything as if he were entirely accustomed to such entertainment. He also appeared to understand and enjoy his host's anecdotes and poetry. When the Raja Sahib threw in a bit of Shakespeare, he confessed frankly that he could not follow it, but when his host translated and explained, he applauded that too, in real appreciation.

After dinner, there was musical entertainment. The male guests adjourned to the main drawing-room, which was an immensely tall room extending the entire height of the house with a glass rotunda. Here they reclined on Bokhara rugs and leaned against silk bolsters. The ladies had been sent home in motorcars. It would not have been fitting for them to be present, because the musicians were not from a respectable class. Only Sofia was emancipated enough to overlook this restriction. At the first party that Bakhtawar Singh attended, the principal singer was a well-known prostitute from Mohabbatpur. She had a strong, well-trained voice, as well as a handsome presence. Bakhtawar Singh did not take his eyes off her. He sat and swayed his head and exclaimed in rapture at her particularly fine modulations. For his sake, she displayed the most delicate subtleties of her art, laying them out like bait to see if he would respond to them, and he

181

cried out as if in passion or pain. Then she smiled. Sofia was also greatly moved. At one point, she turned to Bakhtawar Singh and said, "How good she is." He turned his face to her and nodded, unable to speak for emotion. She was amazed to see tears in his eyes.

Next day she was still thinking about those tears. She told her husband about it, and he said, "Yes, he liked the music, but he liked the singer, too."

"What do you mean?" Sofia asked. When the Raja Sahib laughed, she cried, "Tell me!" and pummelled his chest with her fists.

"I mean," he said, catching her hands and holding them tight, "that they will become friends."

"She will be his mistress?" Sofia asked, opening her eyes wide.

The Raja Sahib laughed with delight. "Where did you learn such a word? In the convent?"

"How do you know?" she pursued. "No, you must tell me! Is he that type of man?"

"What type?" he said, teasing her.

The subject intrigued her, and she continued to think about it to herself. As always when she brooded about anything, she became silent and withdrawn and sat for hours on the veranda, staring out over the dusty plain. "Sofia, Sofia, what are you thinking?" the Raja Sahib asked her. She smiled and shook her head. He looked into her strange, light eyes. There was something mysterious about them. Even when she was at her most playful and affectionate, her eyes seemed always to be looking elsewhere, into some different and distant landscape. It was impossible to tell what she was thinking. Perhaps she was not thinking about anything at all, but the distant gaze gave her the appearance of keeping part

182

of herself hidden. This drove the Raja Sahib crazy with love. He wanted to pursue her into the innermost recesses of her nature, and yet at the same time he respected that privacy of hers and left her to herself when she wanted. This happened often; she would sit and brood and also roam around the house and the land in a strange, restless way. In the end, though, she would always come back to him and nestle against his thin, gray-matted chest and seem to be happy there.

For several days after the party, Sofia was in one of these moods. She wandered around the garden, though it was very hot outside. There was practically no shade, because nothing could be made to grow, for lack of water. She idly kicked at pieces of stone, some of which were broken garden statuary. When it got too hot, she did not return to the house but took shelter in the little ruined fort. It was very dark inside there, with narrow underground passages and winding steep stairs, some of which were broken. Sometimes a bat would flit out from some crevice. Sofia was not afraid; the place was familiar to her. But one day, as she sat in one of the narrow stone passages, she heard voices from the roof. She raised her head and listened. Something terrible seemed to be going on up there. Sofia climbed the stairs, steadying herself against the dank wall. Her heart was beating as loudly as those sounds from above. When she got to the top of the stairs and emerged on to the roof, she saw two men. One of them was Bakhtawar Singh. He was beating the other man, who was also a policeman, around the neck and head with his fists. When the man fell, he kicked him and then hauled him up and beat him more. Sofia gave a cry. Bakhtawar Singh turned his head and saw her. His eyes looked into hers for a moment, and how different they were from that other time when they had been full of tears!

"Get out!" he told the policeman. The man's sobs continued to be heard as he made his way down the stairs. Sofia did not know what to do. Although she wanted to flee, she stood and stared at Bakhtawar Singh. He was quite calm. He put on his khaki bush jacket, careful to adjust the collar and sleeves so as to look smart. He explained that the man had been derelict in his duties and, to escape discipline, had run away and hidden here in the fort. But Bakhtawar Singh had tracked him down. He apologized for trespassing on the Raja Sahib's property and also—here he became courtly and inclined his body toward Sofia—if he had in any way upset and disturbed her. It was not a scene he would have wished a lady to witness.

"There is blood on your hand," she said.

He looked at it. He made a wry face and then wiped it off. (Was it his own or the other man's?) Again he adjusted his jacket, and he smoothed his hair. "Do you often come here?" he asked, indicating the stairs and then politely standing aside to let her go first. She started down, and looked back to see if he was following.

"I come every day," she said.

It was easy for her to go down the dark stairs, which were familiar to her. But he had to grope his way down very carefully, afraid of stumbling. She jumped down the last two steps and waited for him in the open sunlight.

"You come here all alone?" he asked. "Aren't you afraid?"

"Of what?"

He didn't answer but walked round the back of the fort. Here his horse stood waiting for him, grazing among nettles. He jumped on its back and lightly flicked its flanks, and it

184

cantered off as if joyful to be bearing him.

That night Sofia was very restless, and in the morning her face had the clouded, suffering look that presaged one of her attacks. But when the Raja Sahib wanted to darken the room and make her lie down, she insisted that she was well. She got up, she bathed, she dressed. He was surprised—usually she succumbed very quickly to the first signs of an attack—but now she even said that she wanted to go out. He was very pleased with her and kissed her, as if to reward her for her pluck. But later that day, when she came in again, she did have an attack, and he had to sit by her side and hold her hand and chafe her temples. She wept at his goodness. She kissed the hand that was holding hers. He looked into her strange eyes and said, "Sofia, Sofia, what are you thinking?" But she quickly covered her eyes, so that he could not look into them. Then he had to soothe her all over again.

Whenever he had tried to make her see a doctor, she had resisted him. She said all she needed was him sitting by her and she would get well by herself, and it did happen that way. But now she told him that she had heard of a very good doctor in Mohabbatpur, who specialized in nervous diseases. The drive was long and wearying, and she insisted that there was no need for the Raja Sahib to go there with her; she could go by herself, with the car and chauffeur. They had a loving quarrel about it, and it was only when she said very well, in that case she would not go at all, would not take medical treatment, that he gave way. So now once a week she was driven to Mohabbatpur by herself.

The Raja Sahib awaited her homecoming impatiently, and the evenings of those days were like celebrations. They sat on the roof, with candles and wine, and she told him about her drive to Mohabbatpur and what the doctor had said. The Raja Sahib usually had a new passage from his latest blank-verse drama for her to read. She would start off well enough, but soon she would be overcome by laughter and have to hide her face behind the pages of his manuscript. And he would smile with her and say, "Yes, I know, it's all a lot of nonsense."

"No, no!" she cried. Even though she couldn't understand a good deal of what she was reading, she knew that it expressed his romantic nature and his love for her, which were both as deep as a well. She said, "It is only I who am stupid and read so badly." She pulled herself together and went on reading, till made helpless with laughter again.

There was something strange about her laughter. It came bubbling out, as always, as if from an overflow of high spirits, but now her spirits seemed almost too high, almost hysterical. Her husband listened to these new notes and was puzzled by them. He could not make up his mind whether the treatment was doing her good or not.

The Raja Sahib was very kind to his servants, but if any of them did anything to offend him, he was quick to dismiss him. One of his bearers, a man who had been in his employ for twenty years, got drunk one night. This was by no means an unusual occurrence among the servants; the house was in a lonely spot, with no amusements, but there was plenty of cheap liquor available from the village. Usually the servants slept off the effects in their quarters, but this bearer came staggering up on the roof to serve the Raja Sahib and Sofia. There was a scene. He fell and was dragged away by the other servants, but he resisted violently, shouting frightful obscenities, so that Sofia had to put her hands over her ears. The Raja Sahib's face was contorted with fury. The man was dismissed instantly, and when he came back the next day, wretchedly sober, begging pardon and pleading for reinstatement, the Raja Sahib would not hear him. Everyone felt sorry for the man, who had a large family and was, except for these occasional outbreaks, a sober, hardworking person. Sofia felt sorry for him too. He threw himself at her feet, and so did his wife and many children. They all sobbed, and Sofia sobbed with them. She promised to try and prevail upon the Raja Sahib.

She said everything she could—in a rushed, breathless voice, fearing he would not let her finish—and she did not take her eyes off her husband's face as she spoke. She was horrified by what she saw there. The Raja Sahib had very thin lips, and when he was angry he bit them in so tightly that they quite disappeared. He did it now, and he looked so stern and unforgiving that she felt she was not talking to her husband at all but to a gaunt and bitter old man who cared nothing for her. Suddenly she gave a cry, and just as the servant had thrown himself at her feet, so she now prostrated herself at the Raja Sahib's. "Forgive!" she cried. "Forgive!" It was as if she were begging forgiveness for everyone who was weak and had sinned. The Raja Sahib tried to make her rise, but she lay flat on the ground, trying over and over again to bring out the word "Forgive" and not succeeding because of her sobs. At last he managed to help her up; he led her to the bed and waited there till she was calm again. But he was so enraged by the cause of this attack that the servant and his family had to leave immediately.

She always dismissed the car and chauffeur near the doctor's clinic. She gave the chauffeur quite a lot of money—for his food, she said—and told him to meet her in the same place in the evening. She explained that she had to spend the day under observation at the clinic. After the first few times, no explanation was necessary. The chauffeur held out his hand for the money and disappeared until the appointed time. Sofia drew up her sari to veil her face and got into a cycle rickshaw. The place Bakhtawar Singh had chosen for them was a rickety two-storey hotel, with an eating shop downstairs. It was in a very poor, outlying, forgotten part of town, where there was no danger of ever meeting an acquaintance. At first Sofia had been shy about entering the hotel, but as time went on she became bolder. No one ever looked at her or spoke to her. If she was the first to arrive, the key was silently handed to her. She felt secure that the hotel people knew nothing about her, and certainly had never seen her face, which she kept veiled till she was upstairs and the door closed behind her.

In the beginning, he sometimes arrived before her. Then he lay down on the bed, which was the only piece of furniture besides a bucket and a water jug, and was at once asleep. He always slept on his stomach, with one cheek pressed into the pillow. She would come in and stand and look at his dark, muscular, naked back. It had a scar on it, from a knife wound. She lightly ran her finger along this scar, and if that did not wake him, she unwound his loosely tied dhoti, which was all he was wearing. That awakened him immediately.

He was strange to her. That scar on his back was not the only one; there were others on his chest and an ugly long one on his left thigh, sustained during a prison riot. She wanted to know all about his violent encounters, and about his boyhood, his upward struggle, even his low origins. She often asked him about the woman singer at the dinner party. Was it true what the Raja Sahib had said—that he had liked her? Had he sought her out afterward? He did not deny it, but

188

laughed as at a pleasant memory. Sofia wanted to know more and more. What it was like to be with a woman like that? Had there been others? How many, and what was it like with all of them? He was amused by her curiosity and did not mind satisfying it, often with demonstrations.

Although he had had many women, they had mostly been prostitutes and singers. Sometimes he had had affairs with the wives of other police officers, but these too had been rather coarse, uneducated women. Sofia was his first girl of good family. Her refinement intrigued him. He loved watching her dress, brush her hair, treat her skin with lotions. He liked to watch her eat. But sometimes it seemed as if he deliberately wanted to violate her delicacy. For instance, he knew that she hated the coarse, hot lentils that he loved from his boyhood. He would order great quantities, with coarse bread, and cram the food into his mouth and then into hers, though it burned her palate. As their intimacy progressed, he also made her perform acts that he had learned from prostitutes. It seemed that he could not reach far enough into her, physically and in every other way. Like the Raja Sahib, he was intrigued by the look in her foreign eyes, but he wanted to seek out that mystery and expose it, as all the rest of her was exposed to him.

The fact that she was a Muslim had a strange fascination for him. Here too he differed from the Raja Sahib who, as an educated nobleman, had transcended barriers of caste and community. But for Bakhtawar Singh these were still strong. All sorts of dark superstitions remained embedded in his mind. He questioned her about things he had heard whispered in the narrow Hindu alleys he came from—the rites of circumcision, the eating of unclean flesh, what Muslims did with virgin girls. She laughed, never having

189

heard of such things. But when she assured him that they could not be true, he nodded as if he knew better. He pointed to one of his scars, sustained during a Hindu-Muslim riot that he had suppressed. He had witnessed several such riots and knew the sort of atrocities committed in them. He told her what he had seen Muslim men do to Hindu women. Again she would not believe him. But she begged him not to go on; she put her hands over her ears, pleading with him. But he forced her hands down again and went on telling her, and laughed at her reaction. "That's what they did," he assured her. "*Your* brothers. It's all true." And then he struck her, playfully but quite hard, with the flat of his hand.

All week, every week, she waited for her day in Mohabbatpur to come round. She was restless and she began to make trips into the nearby town. It was the usual type of district town, with two cinemas, a jail, a church, temples and mosques, and a Civil Lines, where the government officers lived. Sofia now began to come here to visit the officers' wives whom she had been content to see just once a year at her dinner party. Now she sought them out frequently. She played with their children and designed flower patterns for them to embroider. All the time her thoughts were elsewhere; she was waiting for it to be time to leave. Then, with hurried farewells, promises to come again soon, she climbed into her car and sat back. She told the chauffeur—the same man who took her to Mohabbatpur every week—to drive her through the Police Lines. First there were the policemen's barracks—a row of hutments, where men in vests and shorts could be seen oiling their beards and winding their turbans; they looked up in astonishment from these tasks as her saloon car drove past. She leaned back so as not to be seen, but when they had

190

driven beyond the barracks and had reached the Police Headquarters, she looked eagerly out of the window again. Every time she hoped to get a glimpse of him, but it never happened; the car drove through and she did not dare to have it slow down. But there was one further treat in store, for beyond the offices were the residential houses of the police officers—the Assistant Deputy S.P., the Deputy S.P., the S.P.

One day, she leaned forward and said to the chauffeur, "Turn in."

"In here?"

"Yes, yes!" she cried, mad with excitement.

It had been a sudden impulse—she had intended simply to drive past his house, as usual—but now she could not turn back, she had to see. She got out. It was an old house, built in the times of the British for their own S.P., and now evidently inhabited by people who did not know how to look after such a place. A cow was tethered to a tree on what had once been a front lawn; the verandah was unswept and empty except for some broken crates. The house too was practically unfurnished. Sofia wandered through the derelict rooms, and it was only when she had penetrated to the inner courtyard that the life of the house began. Here there were children and noise and cooking smells. A woman came out of the kitchen and stared at her. She had a small child riding on her hip; she was perspiring, perhaps from the cooking fire, and a few strands of hair stuck to her forehead. She wore a plain and rather dirty cotton sari. She might have been his servant rather than his wife. She looked older than he did, tired and worn out. When Sofia asked whether this was the house of the Deputy S.P., she shook her head wearily, without a smile. She told one of her children to point out the right house, and

191

turned back into her kitchen with no further curiosity. A child began to cry.

At their next meeting, Sofia told Bakhtawar Singh what she had done. He was surprised and not angry, as she had feared, but amused. He could not understand her motives, but he did not puzzle himself about them. He was feeling terribly sleepy; he said he had been up all night (he didn't say why). It was stifling in the hotel room, and perspiration ran down his naked chest and back. It was also very noisy, for the room faced on to an inner yard, which was bounded on its opposite side by a cinema. From noon onward the entire courtyard boomed with the ancient sound track—it was a very poor cinema and could afford to play only very old films—filling their room with Bombay dialogue and music. Bakhtawar Singh seemed not to care about the heat or the noise. He slept through both. He always slept when he was tired; nothing could disturb him. It astonished Sofia, and so did his imperviousness to their surroundings—the horribly shabby room and smell of cheap oil frying from the eating shop downstairs. But now, after seeing his home, Sofia understood that he was used to comfortless surroundings; and she felt so sorry for him that she began to kiss him tenderly while he slept, as if wishing to make up to him for all his deprivations. He woke up and looked at her in surprise as she cried out, "Oh, my poor darling!"

"Why?" he asked, not feeling poor at all.

She began for the first time to question him about his marriage. But he shrugged, bored by the subject. It was a marriage like every other, arranged by their two families when he and his wife were very young. It was all right; they had children—sons as well as daughters. His wife had plenty to do, he presumed she was content—and why shouldn't she

192

be? She had a good house to live in, sufficient money for her household expenses, and respect as the wife of the S.P. He laughed briefly. Yes, indeed, if she had anything to complain of he would like to know what it was. Sofia agreed with him. She even became indignant, thinking of his wife who had all these benefits and did not even care to keep a nice home for him. And not just his home—what about his wife herself? When she thought of that bedraggled figure, more a servant than a wife, Sofia's indignation rose—and with it her tender pity for him, so that again she embraced him and even spilled a few hot tears, which fell on to his naked chest and made him laugh with surprise.

A year passed, and it was again time for the Raja Sahib's annual party. As always, Sofia was terribly excited and began her preparations weeks beforehand. Only this time her excitement reached such a pitch that the Raja Sahib was worried. He tried to joke her out of it; he asked her whom was she expecting, what terribly important guest. Had she invited the President of India, or perhaps the King of Afghanistan? "Yes, yes, the King of Afghanistan!" she cried, laughing but with that note of hysteria he always found so disturbing. Also she lost her temper for the first time with a servant; it was for nothing, for some trifle, and afterward she was so contrite that she could not do enough to make it up to the man.

The party was, as usual, a great success. The Raja Sahib made everyone laugh with his anecdotes, and Bakhtawar Singh also told some stories, which everyone liked. The same singer from Mohabbatpur had been called, and she entertained with the same skill. And again—Sofia watched him—Bakhtawar Singh wept with emotion. She was deeply

193

touched; he was manly to the point of violence (after all, he *was* a policeman), and yet what softness and delicacy there was in him. She revelled in the richness of his nature. The Raja Sahib must have been watching him too, because later, after the party, he told Sofia, "Our friend enjoyed the musical entertainment again this year."

"Of course," Sofia said gravely. "She is a very fine singer."

The Raja Sahib said nothing, but there was something in his silence that told her he was having his own thoughts.

"If not," she said, as if he had contradicted her, "then why did you call for her again this year?"

"But of course," he said. "She is very fine." And he chuckled to himself.

Then Sofia lost her temper with him—suddenly, violently, just as she had with the servant. The Raja Sahib was struck dumb with amazement, but the next moment he began to blame himself. He felt he had offended her with his insinuation, and he kissed her hands to beg her forgiveness. Her convent-bred delicacy amused him, but he adored it too.

She felt she could not wait for her day in Mohabbatpur to come round. The next morning, she called the chauffeur and gave him a note to deliver to the S.P. in his office. She had a special expressionless way of giving orders to the chauffeur, and he a special expressionless way of receiving them. She waited in the fort for Bakhtawar Singh to appear in answer to her summons, but the only person who came was the chauffeur, with her note back again. He explained that he had been unable to find the S.P., who had not been in his office. Sofia felt a terrible rage rising inside her, and she had to struggle with herself not to vent it on the chauffeur. When the man had gone, she sank down against the stone wall and hid her face in her hands. She did not know what was

194

happening to her. It was not only that her whole life had changed; she herself had changed and had become a different person, with emotions that were completely unfamiliar to her.

Unfortunately, when their day in Mohabbatpur at last came around, Bakhtawar Singh was late (this happened frequently now). She had to wait for him in the hot little room. The cinema show had started, and the usual dialogue and songs came from the defective sound track, echoing through courtyard and hotel. Tormented by this noise, by the heat, and by her own thoughts, Sofia was now sure that he was with the singer. Probably he was enjoying himself so much that he had forgotten all about her and would not come.

But he did come, though two hours late. He was astonished by the way she clung to him, crying and laughing and trembling all over. He liked it, and kissed her in return. Just then the sound track burst into song. It was an old favourite—a song that had been on the lips of millions; everyone knew it and adored it. Bakhtawar Singh recognised it immediately and began to sing, "*O my heart, all he has left you is a splinter of himself to make you bleed!*" She drew away from him and saw him smiling with pleasure under his moustache as he sang. She cried out, "Oh, you pig!"

It was like a blow in the face. He stopped singing immediately. The song continued on the sound track. They looked at each other. She put her hand to her mouth with fear—fear of the depths within her from which that word had arisen (never, never in her life had she uttered or thought such abuse), and fear of the consequences.

But after that moment's stunned silence all he did was laugh. He took off his bush jacket and threw himself on the bed. "What is the matter with you?" he asked. "What

195

happened?"

"Oh I don't know. I think it must be the heat." She paused. "And waiting for you," she added, but in a voice so low she was not sure he had heard.

She lay down next to him. He said nothing more. The incident and her word of abuse seemed wiped out of his mind completely. She was so grateful for this that she too said nothing, asked no questions. She was content to forget her suspicions—or at least to keep them to herself and bear with them as best she could.

That night she had a dream. She dreamed everything was as it had been in the first years of her marriage, and she and the Raja Sahib as happy as they had been then. But then one night—they were together on the roof, by candle- and moonlight—he was stung by some insect that came flying out of the food they were eating. At first they took no notice, but the swelling got worse and worse, and by morning he was tossing in agony. His entire body was discoloured; he had become almost unrecognizable. There were several people around his bed, and one of them took Sofia aside and told her that the Raja Sahib would be dead within an hour. Sofia screamed out loud, but the next moment she woke up, for the Raja Sahib had turned on the light and was holding her in his arms. Yes, that very same Raja Sahib about whom she had just been dreaming, only he was not discoloured, not dying, but as he was always—her own husband, with gray-stubbled cheeks and sunken lips. She looked into his face for a moment and, fully awake now, she said, "It's all right. I had a nightmare." She tried to laugh it off. When he wanted to comfort her, she said again, "It's all right," with the same laugh and trying to keep the irritation out of her voice. "Go to sleep," she told him, and pretending to do so herself, she turned on

196

her side away from him.

She continued to be haunted by the thought of the singer. Then she thought, if with one, why not with many? She herself saw him for only those few hours a week. She did not know how he spent the rest of his time, but she was sure he did not spend much of it in his own home. It had had the look of a place whose master was mostly absent. And how could it be otherwise? Sofia thought of his wife—her neglected appearance, her air of utter weariness. Bakhtawar Singh could not be expected to waste himself there. But where did he go? In between their weekly meetings there was much time for him to go to many places, and much time for her to brood.

She got into the habit of summoning the chauffeur more frequently to take her into town. The ladies in the Civil Lines were always pleased to see her, and now she found more to talk about with them, for she had begun to take an interest in local gossip. They were experts on this, and were eager to tell her that the Doctor beat his wife, the Magistrate took bribes, and the Deputy S.P. had venereal disease. And the S.P.? Sofia asked, busy threading an embroidery needle. Here they clapped their hands over their mouths and rolled their eyes around, as if at something too terrible, too scandalous to tell. Was he, Sofia asked—dropping the needle, so that she had to bend down to pick it up again—was he known to be an . . . adventurous person? "Oh! Oh! Oh!" they cried, and then they laughed because where to start, where to stop, telling of *his* adventures?

Sofia decided that it was her fault. It was his wife's fault first, of course, but now it was hers too. She had to arrange to be with him more often. Her first step was to tell the Raja Sahib that the doctor said she would have to attend the clinic several times a week. The Raja Sahib agreed at once. She felt so grateful that she was ready to give him more details, but he cut her short. He said that of course they must follow the doctor's advice, whatever it was. But the way he spoke—in a flat, resigned voice—disturbed her, so that she looked at him more attentively than she had for some time past. It struck her that he did not look well. Was he ill? Or was it only old age? He did look old, and emaciated too, she noticed, with his skinny, wrinkled neck. She felt very sorry for him and put out her hand to touch his cheek. She was amazed by his response. He seemed to tremble at her touch, and the expression on his face was transformed. She took him in her arms. He *was* trembling. "Are you well?" she whispered to him anxiously.

"Oh yes!" he said in a joyful voice. "Very, very well."

She continued to hold him. She said, "Why aren't you writing any dramas for me these days?"

"I will write," he said. "As many as you like." And then he clung to her, as if afraid to be let go from her embrace.

But when she told Bakhtawar Singh that they could now meet more frequently, he said it would be difficult for him. Of course he wanted to, he said—and how much! Here he turned to her and with sparkling eyes quoted a line of verse which said that if all the drops of water in the sea were hours of the day that he could spend with her, still they would not be sufficient for him. "But . . ." he added regretfully.

"Yes?" she asked, in a voice she tried to keep calm.

"Sh-h-h—Listen," he said, and put his hand over her mouth.

There was an old man saying the Muhammedan prayers in the next room. The hotel had only two rooms, one facing the courtyard and the other the street. This latter was usually

198

empty during the day—though not at night—but today there was someone in it. The wall was very thin, and they could clearly hear the murmur of his prayers and even the sound of his forehead striking the ground.

"What is he saying?" Bakhtawar Singh whispered.

"I don't know," she said. The usual—*la illaha il lallah* . . . I don't know."

"You don't know your own prayers?" Bakhtawar Singh said, truly shocked.

She said, "I could come every Monday, Wednesday, and Friday." She tried to make her voice tempting, but instead it came out shy.

"You do it," he said suddenly.

"Do what?"

"Like he's doing," he said, jerking his head toward the other room, where the old man was. "Why not?" he urged her. He seemed to want it terribly.

She laughed nervously. "You need a prayer carpet. And you must cover your head." (They were both stark naked.)

"Do it like that. Go on," he wheedled. "Do it."

She laughed again, pretending it was a joke. She knelt naked on the floor and began to pray the way the old man was praying in the next room, knocking her forehead on the ground. Bakhtawar Singh urged her on, watching her with tremendous pleasure from the bed. Somehow the words came back to her and she said them in chorus with the old man next door. After a while, Bakhtawar Singh got off the bed and joined her on the floor and mounted her from behind. He wouldn't let her stop praying, though. "Go on," he said, and how he laughed as she went on. Never had he had such enjoyment out of her as on that day.

But he still wouldn't agree to meet her more than once a

199

week. Later, when she tried ever so gently to insist, he became playful and said didn't she know that he was a very busy policeman. Busy with what, she asked, also trying to be playful. He laughed enormously at that and was very loving, as if to repay her for her good joke. But then after a while he grew more serious and said, "Listen—it's better not to drive so often through Police Lines."

"Why not?" Driving past his office after her visits to the ladies in the Civil Lines was still the highlight of her expeditions into town.

He shrugged. "They are beginning to talk."

"Who?"

"Everyone." He shrugged again. It was only her he was warning. People talked enough about him anyway; let them have one more thing. What did he care?

"Oh nonsense," she said. But she could not help recollecting that the last few times all the policemen outside their hutments seemed to have been waiting for her car. They had cheered her as she drove past. She had wondered at the time what it meant but had soon put it out of her mind. She did that now too; she couldn't waste her few hours with Bakhtawar Singh thinking about trivial matters.

But she remembered his warning the next time she went to visit the ladies in the Civil Lines. She wasn't sure then whether it was her imagination of whether there really was something different in the way they were with her. Sometimes she thought she saw them turn aside, as if to suppress a smile, or exchange looks with each other that she was not supposed to see. And when the gossip turned to the S.P., they made very straight faces, like people who know more than they are prepared to show. Sofia decided that it was her imagination; even if it wasn't, she could not worry about it. Later, when she drove through the Police Lines, her car was cheered again by the men in underwear lounging outside their quarters, but she didn't trouble herself much about that either. There were so many other things on her mind. That day she instructed the chauffeur to take her to the S.P.'s residence again, but at the last moment—he had already turned into the gate and now had to reverse—she changed her mind. She did not want to see his wife again; it was almost as if she were afraid. Besides, there was no need for it. The moment she saw the house, she realized that she had never ceased to think of that sad, bedraggled woman inside. Indeed, as time passed the vision had not dimmed but had become clearer. She found also that her feelings toward this unknown woman had changed completely, so that, far from thinking about her with scorn, she now had such pity for her that her heart ached as sharply as if it were for herself.

Sofia had not known that one's heart could literally, physically ache. But now that it had begun it never stopped; it was something she was learning to live with, the way a patient learns to live with his disease. And moreover, like the patient, she was aware that this was only the beginning and that her disease would get worse and pass through many stages before it was finished with her. From week to week she lived only for her day in Mohabbatpur, as if that were the only time when she could get some temporary relief from pain. She did not notice that, on the contrary, it was on that day that her condition worsened and passed into a more acute stage, especially when he came late, or was absent-minded, or—and this was beginning to happen too—failed to turn up altogether. Then, when she was driven back home, the pain in her heart was so great that she had to hold her hand there. It seemed to her that if only there were someone,

201

one other living soul, she could tell about it, she might get some relief. Gazing at the chauffeur's stolid, impassive back, she realized that he was now the person who was closest to her. It was as if she had confided in him, without words. She only told him where she wanted to go, and he went there. He told her when he needed money, and she gave it to him. She had also arranged for several increments in his salary.

The Raja Sahib had written a new drama for her. Poor Raja Sahib! He was always there, and she was always with him, but she never thought about him. If her eyes fell on him, either she did not see or, if she did, she postponed consideration of it until some other time. She was aware that there was something wrong with him, but he did not speak of it, and she was grateful to him for not obtruding his own troubles. But when he told her about the new drama he wanted her to read aloud, she was glad to oblige him. She ordered a marvellous meal for that night and had a bottle of wine put on ice. She dressed herself in one of his grandmother's saris, of a gold so heavy that it was difficult to carry. The candles in blue glass chimneys were lit on the roof. She read out his drama with all the expression she had been taught at her convent to put into poetry readings. As usual she didn't understand a good deal of what she was reading, but she did notice that there was something different about his verses. There was one line that read "Oh, if thou didst but know what it is like to live in hell the way I do!" It struck her so much that she had to stop reading. She looked across at the Raja Sahib; his face was rather ghostly in the blue candlelight.

"Go on," he said, giving her that gentle, self-deprecating smile he always had for her when she was reading his dramas.

202

But she could not go on. She thought, what does he know about that, about living in hell? But as she went on looking at him and he went on smiling at her, she longed to tell him what it *was* like.

"What is it, Sofia? What are you thinking?"

There had never been anyone in the world who looked into her eyes the way he did, with such love but at the same time with a tender respect that would not reach farther into her than was permissible between two human beings. And it was because she was afraid of changing that look that she did not speak. What if he should turn aside from her, the way he had when she had asked forgiveness for the drunken servant?

"Sofia, Sofia, what are you thinking?"

She smiled and shook her head and, with an effort went on reading. She saw that she could not tell him but would have to go on bearing it by herself for as long as possible, though she was not sure how much longer that could be.